REA

Bad Trip South

Other Five Star Titles
by Billie Sue Mosiman:

Final Cut

Bad Trip South

Billie Sue Mosiman

Five Star • Waterville, Maine

First Edition
First Printing: February 2004

Published in 2004 in conjunction with Tekno Books and Ed Gorman.

Set in 11 pt. Plantin by Ramona Watson.

Printed in the United States on permanent paper.

ISBN 1-59414-105-3 (hc : alk. paper)

Bad Trip South

At the piping of all hands,
When the judgment signal's spread—
When the islands and the lands
And the seas give up their dead,
And the South and North shall come;
When the sinner is dismayed,
And the just man is afraid,
Then Heaven be thy aid, Poor Tom.

Lament for Long Tom
John Gardiner Calkins Brainard (1795–1828)

The thunder of gunfire filled the weeded area between the abandoned, unpainted house and the line of half a dozen patrol cars. Windows in the house cracked and blew inwards with ear-shattering concussions.

Suddenly the door opened and a little girl came running from the house toward the police cars. She was screaming, her legs pumping, and dark hair flying. Both her arms rotated like pinwheels and from deep in her little chest issued a silent scream. She looked like a ragged street child thrown on the mercy of chance.

All around her the gunfire exploded, with shots coming from both directions, from behind and in front. Miraculously none of the bullets struck her as she rushed forward, her eyes wide in terror and spittle flying from her lips.

She ran until she collapsed into the arms of a man who stepped from cover behind a car where he'd been hunched. He caught her, stumbling back when she barreled directly into his extended arms. He threw her down to the ground behind the trunk of his car.

An order of "Cease fire!" had been called out and yet was not obeyed as soon as she appeared. Now that the child had crossed through Hell and survived it, the gunshots halted. That is, they stopped except for the shots coming from the house where someone at a broken window shouted something unintelligible and fired a handgun over and over, the single shots ringing and echoing loudly up into the cold blue Texas sky, drowning out the little girl's sobbing. . . .

* * * * *

"Can you tell me what happened?" The policeman—a psychologist, he said, a very special kind of policeman—sat back in his chair and took a drag on his cigarette. He squinted one eye as smoke coiled lazily past his brow.

I kept glancing around and fidgeting in my chair just like I always did in the doctor's office when I was a little kid. Only this wasn't a doctor's office and this wasn't my hometown. And the man at the desk wasn't going to give me a magic shot to make it all right.

I was used to a little town and a little reception area where the sheriff sat behind his desk reading Burpee seed catalogs and *Field and Stream*. Nothing like this place.

Outside the office I could hear the noise of the station where at least a dozen people worked. There were policemen answering telephones, lawyers talking to people who had been arrested, illegal aliens pleading in their own language, and, out on the street, the whole city making noises like a country band I'd seen once up on the platform in the gazebo in the middle of our town. They had a tambourine player, a man on a washboard, a drummer, banjo and guitar players. That band and this place made me want to put my hands up to flip down my ears and press them hard against the side of my head to make the sounds go away.

It wasn't the policeman's fault. All the noise. He didn't know how nervous it made me. I liked him a lot. Although he said he'd worked with my Daddy back in North Carolina, this was the first time I'd ever met him. Who would have thought he'd be all the way down here in Brownsville, Texas? But then who would have thought I'd be here either? I could tell he was sorry about everything and how I had to talk to him.

He looked like Captain Kangaroo, but a lot younger. Bushy gray eyebrows stuck out over his eyes and his face was round, his mouth about to break into a smile, but didn't quite. His eyes didn't match his face. They were the kind of eyes Daddy got when he had a suspect in his squad car, questioning him. Real serious. No fun. Fun was a long way off from eyes like that.

This man had been a police psychologist a long time, I could tell. He was probably more of a policeman than he was anything else, sort of like my Daddy was in the beginning, back when I was a really little kid.

I locked my hands together so I wouldn't bend down my ears, and asked, Where do you want me to start?

He took the cigarette from his lips between thumb and forefinger, like hoody boys do on TV shows, and waved it in semi-circles toward me. "How about from the beginning? I have plenty of time, little lady."

I tried to smile because he was trying to be nice, but I wasn't a lady yet. Mama's a lady. You have to be over twenty years old to be a lady and I'm only ten.

He was waiting for me to say something, though, so I told him. . . .

. . . When Daddy turned into the parking lot for the Long Horn Caverns outside of St. Louis, I knew he was only doing it for Mom and me. To make up for the fight they'd had outside of Memphis where Mom let slip what she planned to do after our trip. She was taking me to Grand's and moving out for good. She was divorcing him.

I knew that already so I wasn't surprised, but when she said it to Daddy, his voice got deep scratchy, like one of those old record albums Mama let me have. I wasn't surprised because I'd heard her talking to Grand when I was supposed to be packing for the trip the week we left North Carolina. Then Mama caught me eavesdropping and set me down for a talk. I knew it was really serious when we had to have a talk. Parents don't take much time with kids for real, grown-up conversations, unless it's serious.

I was kind of relieved after I tiptoed to the doorway and listened. I'm going to miss Daddy, I thought, but we have to get out before something terrible happens.

It was really hot that day in the car, driving into the big parking lot for the Long Horn Caverns. So hot the air conditioner on our new car Daddy had just bought couldn't cool us down.

I paused, looking at the nice psychologist. It's a long story, I said. Are you sure I should tell you everything?

He waved me on again. He'd lit another cigarette. I don't mind cigarette smoke. Most kids do, they make a big deal of it, coughing and stuff, but I'm used to it. It makes me feel at home. Daddy smoked Kent, the long skinny ones, before he quit when I was eight. I still sort of missed the smell. I knew when he was in the house when he used to smoke. I could detect him without hearing his voice or his heavy footsteps.

Anyway, Daddy drove into the Long Horn Caverns' entrance and said, "You'll like this, Em." He turned off the ignition and almost instantly hot air from outside the car made the air inside feel stuffy and too close. He'd parked in

10

front of the caverns and now opened his car door. Then the heat outside whooshed inside in one big heavy wave that smacked me right in the face.

I'd like anything better than sitting in the car where it was so ugly quiet, them not speaking to one another. Mama never talked back to him. If she did, the ugly quiet turned to screaming and hitting. Daddy hitting her.

I could smell something awful burning when they fought, like plastic or rubber, but I knew it was my imagination. Nothing was burning but the two people in the front seat. Daddy had been bad for a long time. He hadn't raised a hand to me, but he'd hurt Mom more than once. It was hard loving him. I think some grown people are real hard to love even when you're supposed to and you want to.

"You know what I mean?" I asked the nice psychologist.

He said he knew. He knew that for sure. And he added, "Even when you get grown up, sometimes it's hard to love people when you think you should."

I wanted to think about that. No one had ever told me that secret before about grown-ups. But he was waving me on so I put my head back against the chair and looked up at the ceiling until I could see the caverns again, that cool, dark entrance in the side of the hill. All I could think about that day was how cool it must be underground and how fast I wanted us to walk through the boiling sunlight to get down there in the caves.

As soon as I was out on the scorching parking lot, shading my eyes to see the promise of the cool caves ahead, I noticed that man.

Crow.

They called him Scarecrow in prison, but that didn't fit him, he said, he wasn't like no old damn raggedy-butt suit hung out on a cross in a field. So we called him Crow.

He wore black, like a crow's feathers. I thought he ought to wear shirts, because he had a chest that showed his ribs, and it was too white, like bread dough, but that day he only had on a black leather vest over black denim jeans. His belt had a round polished brass buckle that glinted golden and shiny as a mirror.

He stood near the store entrance where you went to buy tickets for a tour of the caves. He watched us, not even moving a muscle. Just watching. I didn't like his eyes at all. They kept secrets. They were thinking about something that wasn't nice and it involved us.

Then, as we started across the parking lot to where he stood, a girl came out of the store and stood next to him. She slipped her arm around his waist and leaned on him. He didn't do much, just let her. He was still watching us, too busy to think of the girl.

She had on real short shorts, cut-off blue jean shorts, and her legs were long and brown, like an Indian's. Her hair was long too, the color of wheat that goes dry in the fields. It hung straight down around her shoulders all the way to her waist. I thought she was way too pretty to like a skinny guy like Crow, but you could tell she really did like him. She was whispering in his ear when we got to the store and passed them by.

When we got closer, I didn't think the girl pretty any-more. She had something wrong with her mouth. One side of it pulled down so that she talked out the other side. Like old people, when they get sick and sit in wheelchairs and they can't lift one of their arms or move one of their legs. Only the girl could move her arms and legs. Her mouth was just funny. Almost scary, like a dream that's all crooked and doesn't make any sense, but you know it means something if you could only figure it out.

12

Mama and Daddy paid them no mind, but I stared at them hard. I did that because Crow had been staring at us and it's not polite to stare. He smelled like swamp water, though I might have been the only one to notice. He smelled like water sitting still in dark shade, with worms wiggling in it and dead frogs floating on top.

I think he hissed when we went through the door, but no one heard it but me. I might have imagined that too, the same as the smells. And I thought I heard him whisper, "They're the ones."

Or maybe he didn't say it; I just read his mind. I don't . . . you know . . . expect you'll understand this—or believe me. But it's true. I just seem to know what people are thinking. I've never figured out why other people don't know how to do it because it seems easy. You just look someone in the eye and you can nearly tell what's in his head. Even when a person doesn't want you to know.

Kids' minds are better at surprising you than grown-ups'. I almost always know what grown-ups are really thinking. Kids think crazy stuff so you can't figure them out that easy. Their thoughts leapfrog all over the place and hardly make any good sense at all.

As soon as I heard Crow say we were the ones, I looked up at Daddy to see if he heard, and I knew he hadn't, that maybe Crow hadn't said it out loud. I should tell him, that's what I thought, I need to tell him the boy and the girl at the door want something from us. But Daddy's mouth was in that tight line it gets when he's still mad. And Mama was already off to the souvenir counter, looking at silver bracelets and earrings with dangling feathers and rings with turquoise chips in them. She liked stuff like that. She wore a turquoise pinkie ring she'd gotten in Tennessee. Daddy had never really bought her nice jewelry—you know, the gold kind with diamonds and all—couldn't afford it, he said.

Maybe if I'd told Daddy about Crow, if I'd taken the chance on Daddy getting mad and yelling at me, nothing ever would have happened. Daddy had his service revolver along in the car. He had his badge in his wallet.

He could have arrested them. For something. For staring like that. For wanting to use us that way. At least he would have been ready for what happened when we came out of the cave tour.

And I wouldn't be here now having to tell you how all the bad things happened.

And I wouldn't have to listen to this noise, I thought, watching the nice detective now instead of the ceiling. Because I wouldn't be here in a big border city police station, all alone, so awfully all alone.

* * * * *

"They're the ones," Crow said. "Got a nice car. They come out of the tour, we'll take the keys."

Heddy glanced from beneath her silvery blond lashes at the sun beating down on the parking lot. It seemed to her it was pouring like hot lava over the cars. She frowned, feeling a trickle of sweat start down her spine. She really hated getting all sweaty and smelling like a crate of dead fish.

It was the middle of the week, not many tourists at the caverns. Only three vehicles were parked out front. Two of them looked too old and beat up to make it to the state line.

She felt a lust start up in her heart for the shiny new Buick Riviera the family owned. Leather seats . . . cold blasts of air conditioning . . . power windows . . . stereo speakers . . . They must have money. What could it be like to have money like that? The car cost more than any house Heddy had ever lived in. Just about any new car today cost more than the shacks she'd had to call home. Right now her mom lived in a green and white thirty-four-foot trailer that she'd picked up for five hundred bucks and a blowjob she gave the crippled owner who said he was dying anyway, take the damn trailer, what the hell good was it to him? It was shabby and full of termites, but it was probably the best "house" Heddy had ever stayed in.

"We can wait for those people to come out of the caverns if the search party doesn't find us first," she said now, forcibly bringing her attention back to the problem at hand.

"You think they're this close?" Crow shivered a little, as if the fear he'd kept at bay for hours when they'd been on the run had returned, crawling up his back to sink pinchers into the base of his neck.

Heddy seemed to be reading the clouds. She hugged his waist tighter, snuggling her shoulder into his armpit. He didn't smell good, particularly, but he smelled like a man and she loved the smell of men, no matter how sweaty. "It only took us an hour to get here by foot. They'll find the car, and then they'll head here, just like we did. If they can follow us across the state, they can follow us here. We don't have a lot of time."

Crow swung his large black leather satchel bag around to the front of him and patted it. "Where'd you get the piece?"

"Bandy. He said it shot good. The one I have shoots good too."

15

"Well, we know they shoot good, don't we? You pay him?"

Heddy squirmed away and picked at a line of freckles that marched up her left arm.

"I said, did you pay him? I guess no answer means you paid him on your fucking back. I never trusted Bandy. He'd steal gold from a dead man's teeth."

"What's it matter how I paid him, we got the guns, didn't we? And I was waiting when you skipped, wasn't I? Who's your baby? Who's always there for you?"

Crow smiled a rare smile, this one dripping with the lust he felt for the girl. "Yeah, you're my baby. I'd still be back in that cell, wasn't for you."

She snuggled into his arm again, breathing deeply and smiling all inside just to be in the circle of his scent. "We have to take that family with us. That's what we have to do."

"Why the hell would we want to do that?" He glared down at her, his black brows knitting together. He knew she was smarter than he was, but it still burned him up when she came up with stuff he hadn't thought of. She knew that, but there wasn't much she could change about the arrangement. She made the plans. She called the shots. That's how it had to be.

"We just grab the car, we won't make it to the line. They'll tell, Crow. They saw us. They can describe us. Then the cops will know what kind of car we're driving. On the other hand, if we grab the mom, pop, and kid, they're insurance. We can drop them off somewhere, after we're far away from here. I don't want you put back in prison. We can't take chances, no chances. I've got you now, I don't want them taking you away again."

"Yeah, I can see that. Hell. Company. I didn't really want company around. Who's gonna drive?"

16

She kissed him, nibbling softly on his bottom lip. She said, "I will. You sit in back with the gun on the kid. Everything will be fine. We'll be on the other side of Missouri by dark."

"God." He sucked in her lip, then covered her whole mouth, twirling his tongue around hers until she felt the beginning of his erection. She gently disengaged, pushing him back. He was breathing hard. "I don't know if I can wait," he said.

She reached down, patted the bulge in the crotch of his jeans. "Yes, you can. You've waited for four years already."

* * * * *

Daddy bought the tour tickets and called Mama over to join the guide. Crow and his girlfriend didn't go on the tour. They were still outside, by the door, like they were waiting for a ride to pick them up. I know now they were waiting for us to get through the caverns and leave so they could get the car.

There was one other couple who went on the tour with us, an old man and woman who walked real slow. I tried to listen to the guide, a pretty girl with a turned-up nose who looked like a high school cheerleader in her tight uniform. She told us about the caves and the story how outlaws hid out in it a long time ago, and before that, how the Indians held powwows in the caves, burning fires, eating antelope and buffalo. I tried to listen, but I kept looking back behind us, thinking Crow would be there, so I missed a lot of what the girl guide said.

It was cold and got colder in the caves as we walked through them. There were little lights along the pathway and more lights shining on some of the walls and the ceiling. The air was thick with damp and smelled like a grave deep, deep, deep down in the earth. Those stalag . . . things hung from the ceiling, like swords about to drop, and they stuck up from the floor, like tall muddy anthills. I would have thought it was neat except I couldn't stop worrying.

I tugged on Mama's hand and whispered, "Did you see that man when we came in?" She shushed me because the girl guide was talking about Old West outlaws. She didn't even hear what I said. Mama's a schoolteacher and she doesn't like me to interrupt when people are talking. Especially when they're teaching you stuff.

Toward the end of the tour, I got near Daddy and took his hand. He looked down at me and smiled a little. I said, "Daddy, there was a man watching us when we got here."

He said, "Is that right?" But he wasn't really paying attention. He kept watching the girl guide as she walked ahead of us, swinging her flashlight around the cave walls. He thought she was pretty. He watched her bottom and hardly ever blinked.

Mama didn't care—though I think she noticed it too—but I wished Daddy wouldn't look at girls that way with Mama right beside him. He used to think Mama was the prettiest girl there was. He was jealous of her and some of his fits came from thinking she would like someone else better than him. But now he liked how the girl guide looked so much he hardly knew Mama was alive. He wasn't listening to how important it was Crow was watching us and talking about us when we walked inside.

Realizing Daddy wasn't going to hear what I said either, I dropped his hand and hung back, following both my parents while I chewed the inside of my lip. All I could do was hope Crow wasn't there when we came out of the caves. Maybe he'd change his mind and find someone else to bother. Maybe he'd already found someone and they'd left. I could have, well . . . listened in to his mind to find out if he'd left, but I really didn't want to do that. For some reason I knew I wouldn't like what I'd find inside his head. Just looking at him and catching little stray thoughts from him was bad enough. I sure didn't want to go looking into his thoughts if I didn't have to.

I've seen bad people before. That's something you have to know about me. I might be ten, but I'm pretty old for a little kid. Probably because all these years I've heard grown-ups talk in their heads and I know stuff other kids just don't know. That's how I knew something was wrong with Crow and Heddy. I knew they were bad people. Heddy, that was her name, Crow's girlfriend. She was just as bad as Crow, that was obvious to me the minute I walked past her and saw her funny mouth, and her eyes that were shiny and trying to be normal, but weren't normal at all because they let too much of her *out* when she looked at you.

I think sometimes Daddy turned bad from being around so many bad people. It's like getting sick. You catch stuff from people, colds and the flu and measles. If you're only around bad people, maybe you catch what they have that makes them that way. Daddy had to arrest drunks and thieves and a couple of times he even arrested killers. Sonny and Jimmy Cochran, two brothers who shaved their heads and wore sleeveless tee shirts. "Stone killers" Daddy called them. They broke into old Mrs. Lampisi's house one night real late, thinking she'd stay sleeping. When she got up and surprised them, they beat her to death with their fists and kicked her a lot. It was the big Army boots they wore that probably killed her. I don't like to even think about it. Daddy didn't know I knew about them, but it was in the newspapers, pictures with their bald heads shining like wet grapes and their eyes—real cold and hard looking, like people who don't care about living anymore. Eyes like Heddy had.

Daddy had once been a policeman in Charlotte for two years before I was born, and he used to talk about that at the kitchen table with Mama, how awful it was on the street, how lowdown, he said, people could be. "And they're no damn better in a little town," he said, like he was biting down on a bitter lemon.

I don't guess all policemen get infected like Daddy did, but that's what happened. Like something in his head turned sour and he had to take it out on someone. Mama was handy, she was the goat. Isn't that what they call it? The goat that gets all the blame?

If Daddy had been watching when we went into the caves he would have known how bad Crow and Heddy were, but this time he just wasn't all there. He was thinking about Mama leaving him and taking me away. He was fuming, like a volcano, heating up to the point he'd blow. He couldn't see anything or anybody, but the way the house would be empty back in our town when we got home from the vacation.

Then he could only see the girl guide, in her brown pants uniform, pretty and young like my Barbie dolls. All blonde and perfect, dolly-like. If she had been my Barbie, I'd have put a shiny black ballgown on her and red high heels on her little feet.

That's how Crow surprised my Daddy, taking advantage of a man who isn't thinking straight.

We came from the tour, our eyes watering in the sunlight after being down in the dark caves, and before we were halfway across the parking lot, Crow came up behind my Daddy and said, "Don't give me any trouble if you want your kid to live."

He had one hand on my shoulder, pushing me along. His hand felt tough, hard, and mean, like if it had teeth, it'd bite me. I saw Mama's mouth drop open. She said, "Jay . . . ?" Suddenly Heddy was beside her, taking her arm, talking to her so softly I couldn't hear what she was saying.

Daddy looked over at me and I saw in his eyes he remembered what I'd said during the tour. About the man watching us. And he was sorry, then, and angry, because now he was helpless to stop what was happening.

He tried anyway. Daddy was turning into a bad man, but he still loved us. He still knew what was right and wrong.

"Take your hand off my daughter. What do you think you're doing?"

Crow stepped over close to Daddy, pulling me along with him, his fingers digging like claws into my shoulder. He opened his leather bag enough so Daddy could see his hand on the gun in there.

"Get in the front seat of the car," Crow said. "Just do what I say."

That's how it started.

Frank Hawkins let the little girl go to the bathroom. While she was out of the interrogation room, he thought about the story she'd told him. He thought about Jay and how he might have let the family get kidnapped.

Although Frank knew more about Jay Anderson than just about anyone, he thought maybe Jay's daughter knew him from the heart out. Jay had been coming to Frank for six months prior to the vacation that ended in abduction and death. Problem at home, problem with his wife. Once the sessions got into it, Frank discovered it wasn't a wife problem, it was purely a Jay Anderson problem. It was like other cases Frank had seen and dealt with before in his years as a psychologist on the force. Jay—just as the girl said—turned bad. He took the violence from the street home with him. It altered his relationship with his wife to the point there was no love left, only recrimination, sadness, loneliness, and, ultimately, danger.

Jay had said in an early session, "I don't know why the sheriff's sent me to you. I got to drive all the way down here to Charlotte for this? It's crazy. It's wasting your time and mine. There's nothing wrong with me."

"You don't think you're out of control?" Frank had asked.

"Hell no!" With that outburst, Jay bit his lip and looked down where he rubbed together the knuckles of his hands in nervousness. "I don't know," he amended. "Maybe I am."

It grew apparent the more Frank saw of Jay that the man was in trouble, double-digit, inflationary trouble. Not only was he using his badge of authority to manhandle some of his arrested suspects, but also he took all his frustration out on his family when he went home.

Frank did not altogether dislike his patient. Yes, he was a wife beater and, yes, he probably should resign from police work, but he really was struggling to come to terms with what he had become. After denials and a few rants, Jay hung his head in shame, admitting he was abusive. He was angry. He might explode and really do great harm if Frank didn't help him. "I don't want to do that," he'd said. "I couldn't live with myself if I did something . . . permanent."

It was the first step to redemption. And it was as far as they'd gotten after six months before Jay announced he was going on a two-week vacation with his family.

Frank advised against it. Stopping in the middle of therapy wasn't a good idea. Too many parts of Jay's personality were unresolved. Couldn't he put off the vacation for another time?

Jay was adamant. He was going. He and his wife were about to break up and the vacation might cool things off. He needed the time away from work. He was having trouble concentrating, trouble sleeping. If he didn't take this time, not only would he lose his marriage, but he also might make some serious mistakes at work and then where would he be? They'd pick up the therapy where they left off when he got back, he said.

Frank okayed it with Jay's superior despite his better judgment. What could he do, handcuff the man in his office, force therapy on him?

Yet whenever Frank thought about Jay during the two-week lapse between sessions, he wished he'd held against the idea. The thought of Jay on the road with his wife and child, his life dribbling by in unstructured hours, put Frank into an agitated, anxious state. How was it going? Was the wife all right? Was Jay, not ever a patient man, losing it out there in some motel or roadside inn?

That was why when Jay didn't return for his scheduled visit after his vacation, Frank started investigating why. Jay was a potential bomb walking around loose. And where was he? Where was his family?

Frank started looking into it. He knew immediately

something was terribly wrong. He just had no idea where to start looking. It wasn't until several days after the family had already been in the clutches of the violent pair known as Crow and Heddy that Frank got a break.

Emily returned from the bathroom, opening the door to the interrogation office slowly, peeking shyly around the door at him. She came forward slowly and took the chair opposite the desk.

She was such a great kid. She wasn't pretty or anything, but there was an intelligence in her eyes that made you want to hunker down and have a little conversation with her. She wore her hair short and straight, with brown bangs that came below her eyebrows and from which she glanced up through when she had her head down talking about things that might even make an adult embarrassed to discuss. Her voice was soft and steady, rarely breaking, and she didn't cry. He knew when this little girl was grown, she was going to be someone exceptional and she might even do great things in the world. Though she claimed she could read minds, he tried not to scoff or let on the whole notion was too bizarre for words. She believed it and that's what counted.

Besides, though he didn't believe in such matters, he was open to proof, if there was verification. If she continued the story of the abduction and could show she really knew what people thought, well . . . well, he didn't know what he'd think about it then.

There were a great many mysteries in the world and humans were the most mysterious creatures ever to live. In his capacity as a police psychologist, he had come across a great many more unbelievable claims than telepathy. One officer in therapy had sworn on his mother's life that he saw ghosts. All the time. Especially down in one section of

Charlotte near the graveyard when he drove past in his patrol car. They swarmed the street and climbed over his car, he said. They shook their heads, moaning and pointing, and he did not know what in the world they wanted with him. It was to the point he couldn't drive that route anymore. If he had to make a call, he made a wide circuit, avoiding the streets surrounding the cemetery, even if it meant taking longer to get to his destination. No amount of rational therapy he was given could convince him otherwise. There were ghosts; he saw them; that was the end of it.

Frank looked at Emily and smiled to put her at ease again. She was the only one with all the pieces to the Anderson puzzle. He wondered if she could read *his* mind. If so she'd know his thoughts about how lucky she was to have come through the joyride alive.

* * * * *

Crow waited until Heddy had the keys and was behind the wheel. He waited until the man was in the front tan-leather bucket seat beside her, with the mother and kid in the back seat. Then he got in the back next to the kid. He pulled out the gun then and let them see it. "I got nothing to lose," he said. "Anyone interfere with Heddy's driving and the kid says good-bye, world, *adios, muchacho*."

"Tell us what's going on," the man said.

"What's your name?" Crow leaned up toward the front seat and looked at him hard while Heddy got the car started. She pulled away from the parking lot onto the road leading away from the Long Horn Caverns.

"Jay Anderson."

"What kind of name is that, Jay? That's a fag name, it's a woman's name. Jay, Jayne, Joyce. You're not a Jason, are you? I knew a Jason once, hated the fuck."

"Not a Jason. Just Jay."

Crow sat back, turned to the woman. "And what's your name and the kid's name?"

"I'm Carrie. This is Emily."

He liked how her voice wavered. She looked scared enough to piss her pants.

"One big happy family," Heddy said from the driver's seat. "God, this is a beautiful car."

"I'm called Crow and this here's Heddy. You just do what we say and it's all going to be all right."

"If you want the car, why don't you . . . ?"

Crow leaned forward again to the man and lashed him on the cheek with the gun barrel. The man screeched and blood started running down from the cut on the cheekbone. The woman screamed and the little girl jumped like a live wire had been plugged into her ears.

Heddy said, "Take it easy, Crow. I'm driving here."

Jay got the pocket compartment open and that's when Crow saw the gun. He was halfway over the seat then, reaching out. Heddy started hitting the brakes, pulling to the side of the road, the car swerving in loose gravel before it came to a shuddering stop. Crow stuck his own gun into the man's neck, grinding it in. "Gimme that!"

Jay carefully withdrew the service revolver and handed it over.

"Bad move, man. I coulda blown your brains out. That what you want, me to blow out your brains right in front of your kid and ole lady?"

Jay put his hand to his face where it was swelling now and turning blue. His hand came away red and sticky. "Can I get some napkins from the console here?"

"I'm talking to you! I'm asking you a question!"

"No," Jay said between clenched teeth. "I do not want you to blow my brains out."

"That's smart thinking. You happen to have any other guns stashed in here?"

"No."

Crow turned the gun over in his palm, scrutinizing it. "Looks like a cop's gun. Regulation issue, Smith and Wesson. You a cop?"

"No."

Crow turned to the woman, Carrie. "He's a cop, ain't he? He's got the look. He's got the haircut. He even smells like a stinking cop. I look around, I'm gonna find a badge, right?"

The woman was crying into her hands. She started to shake her head when the kid piped up, "My Daddy'll put you in jail. You can't hit my Daddy like that."

Crow grinned. He slipped the revolver in his satchel. "Only the kid knows how to tell the truth. I'm gonna remember that."

"Oh shit," Heddy said, looking out the side window.

"No big deal," Crow said. "He don't scare me. You think you scare me, cop?"

"The fucking luck," Heddy said. "We have to pick up a cop's family."

"Get the car back on the road, the excitement's over," Crow said. "And don't worry about Jay. He's gonna play nice, aren't you, Jaybird, old boy? Cause I have your gun. And I have your kid back here. And you're not making no more dumb moves, right?"

"Right."

Heddy let up on the brake and eased back onto the road. "The fucking luck," she repeated. "We must be under a bad moon."

* * * * *

I've seen bad moons. They're always the full ones. The big fat yellow ones that drive people crazy. Daddy says when there's a full moon the loonies come out. He never seemed to notice he went loony too when the moon turned full. He'd come home with mad on his face and his eyes all narrow, talking about how many bills he had to pay, and how he wasn't ever going to be more than a patrol officer in our dumpy town, he'd never make detective. How he was sick of the scum, the gangs starting up in town, the whining business owners who wanted him to patrol their properties like he had nothing better to do, like he was a *security officer* instead of a cop. How he should have learned some other job, he hated this job; this job was for common idiots.

Mama would stay clear of him and try to sit quietly at the kitchen table, grading papers from school, but he wanted her to say something. Agree with him, that's what he wanted.

He'd stand right behind her, talking loud. He'd send me to my room, like he couldn't stand looking at me. I think he did that because he knew I knew he was being bad again. Sometimes he was sorry later and I'd hear him begging Mama to forgive him, but he never really meant it. She knew that. So did I. Still, he never stopped doing it.

He'd put ice in a towel and put it on Mama's bruises so they wouldn't swell and he'd say, almost crying, "I don't know what gets in me, Carrie. I'm a lousy son of a bitch, I know I am. When I think about what I do to you, I want to stuff my gun in my mouth."

Then Mama would say, "Don't talk that way, Jay. You can't help it. Things just get inside you and hurt."

I'd look outside from the window seat in my room where I'd be all scrunched up, holding my knees, and I'd see the bad moon high in the sky above our little town and I'd know he was one of those loonies he said made mischief. And he didn't even know. Mama must have known, even when she made excuses for him. But Daddy just had no idea.

Anyway, this was daytime when Heddy said what she did and she couldn't know if there was a bad moon out or not. She just meant it was bad luck, getting in a cop's car, and hitting him with a gun. I was hoping it would be *real bad luck* for them.

Heddy didn't talk a lot. She drove. I think she was bothered by her mouth too, the half of it that didn't work right. She didn't like anyone looking at it when she was talking. She'd give you a mean look, a really evil look, if she caught you watching her mouth when she talked. When she did that, she scared me more than Crow did. I always had to look away so she wouldn't think I was watching her mouth.

Crow talked all the time. He talked too much. He said you couldn't say much in prison, it was too dangerous. People would get you for talking, either the guards or the cons, so you had to keep your trap shut. That's probably why he talked so much now he had escaped. He had a lot of words saved up.

It was Daddy who knew about that. The escape.

We were on the freeway again, heading west into the sun, when Daddy said, "You must have broke out of Leavenworth. If you headed east to St. Louis, why head west now?"

"You've been listening to your radio," Crow said, uncaring.

"You won't get far going west, back toward Kansas."

"Shut up," Heddy said. "If we don't get out of this state, neither will you. It's none of your business what direction we head."

Daddy looked over his shoulder at us. He gave Crow a mean look. I sucked in my breath because his face was getting puffy and his eye was closing. He looked like some kind of monster from a really bad horror movie.

"How do you think we'll get past the roadblocks?" Daddy asked.

"What roadblocks?"

Daddy turned around and stared out the windshield. "They might put up roadblocks," he said nonchalantly.

"He's lying," Heddy said. "He's heard it on the radio. They've got up roadblocks, Crow. God*damn*."

Crow settled against the seat, thinking. "We need to get off the freeway. Find some little road. . . ."

Heddy took the next exit, swerving enough that Crow leaned over on me. I pulled away and got closer to Mama. I could feel her, all trembly, scared the way she was when Daddy was bad.

We pulled into a gas station where Heddy parked in back, away from the pumps. A man was putting air in his tires from the air machine, but he didn't look at us. "We need a map," Heddy said.

"Check where he had the gun," Crow said.

Heddy opened the pocket compartment and rummaged in it. She pulled out a folded United States map. "Here's one."

Mama hadn't said anything since we'd gotten into the car. She said now, "I need to go to the bathroom."

"Hold it," Heddy said. "No one's getting out of the car."

Crow dug in his leather bag and brought out a pack of Wrigley's peppermint gum. He unwrapped a piece and I watched him fold it into his mouth. I wanted to go to the bathroom too all of a sudden, but I knew there was no use saying so. Heddy really meant the stuff she said.

Heddy glanced up from the map. "Okay, we can catch 94 along the Missouri River to Jefferson City. I don't think they'll block that one."

"We should have headed across Kansas when we had the chance." Crow sounded sulky.

"You'd already be caught by now if we had. Besides, we needed . . . you know what we needed in St. Louis, Crow, don't start bitching."

"There was a search party in the woods near the caves, wasn't there?" Daddy asked, brightening.

"Shut up," Heddy said again. She put the map away and got the car on the road.

Daddy knew he'd made a mistake talking about the roadblocks. If he hadn't said anything, they wouldn't have thought of it and maybe we would have been stopped somewhere on the interstate system. Now we were going down through thick forests to a curvy little two-lane highway, Heddy driving too fast.

That made Crow happy. He chewed his gum with his mouth open—really bad manners—and kept looking out the window, grinning.

Daddy just sat like a stone in the front seat, quiet and

cold, moving nothing but his eyes. Mama held my hand and squeezed it so tight my bones mashed together. We all knew it was going to be a long trip. Maybe even into the night.

* * * * *

"Hell, Crow, they've got a CD player in this thing. Can you feature it?"

Crow scooted up to look over the seat then sat back again. "Play something."

Heddy looked over at Jay. "Where's your CDs?"

"We don't have any. We just got the car last week."

"Goddamn it. That's what I was afraid of. You could have bought some Doors stuff or the Eagles or something. Shit."

"Just turn on the radio, Baby." Crow slipped his hand into the leather bag he kept on his lap and took out a foil packet. He unfolded it carefully and jiggled around the little dirty looking crystals there. Then he pulled out a straw cut in half and snorted the crystals up one nostril and then the other. He felt the little girl watching him. Her gaze made his neck prickle.

"You want a hit, kid?" He held out the foil packet toward her and laughed. She withdrew toward her mother like an octopus pulling in its tentacles.

Carrie said, "Leave her alone."

"Leave her alone," Crow mimicked. "Leave my baby alone. Like that kid ain't seen this shit in the schoolyard. Don't get on that high and mighty horse with me."

"Just leave her alone."

32

He stared at her hard until she turned to the window.

Heddy kept scanning radio stations. Light and dark whipped across the interior of the car as they drove down curving roads bounded on both sides with tall green trees. They weren't pines, that's all he knew. The trunks were thick and scaly as the backs of fabled dragons and the canopies were lush with blankets of leaves in mint, emerald, and forest green.

Crow closed his eyes on the blinking light floating over him and let the rush come. It slipped up his diaphragm into his chest until his heart was stomping like a flamenco dancer.

Best thing about Leavenworth was the drugs. You could get anything and everything if you had something of value to exchange. Hell, you could get champagne and caviar if you could pay to get it inside. He wouldn't tell Heddy his big bargaining power rode below his belt. She'd call him a queer, but that's because she didn't know what it was like inside. There were a few real queers, sure, but most of them were like Crow—selling all they had to sell and that was the flesh. In other worlds you lived other lives. Behind the walls, you grabbed your balls. No shit, Sherlock.

When he first got put in Leavenworth, a big nigger, black as midnight and wild as a train off its tracks, came to him and said, "You toss my salad, I'll protect you from the others." Tossing a salad didn't sound too bad to him, but that was before he knew it meant getting down and licking out the guy's asshole until he got off his rocks. The Mod Squad, what the big nigger called himself, stuffed it with strawberry jelly from the breakfast tray and told Crow to lick till he saw stars. So Crow spread the cheeks, shut his eyes and licked for all he was worth. What was he going to do, kill the motherfucker, him weighing two-forty and Crow barely busting scale at one-thirty?

If Heddy knew he'd sucked ass, she'd never kiss him again.

Hell, he wasn't sure he'd blame her either. But that's how he survived prison life, tossing salads, eating bungholes, staying alive, man, drawing breath the best way he knew how.

Four years. Four interminably long years punctuated by night sweats and the horror of the endless routine of the days.

He had tried stuff in prison he wouldn't have gone near on the street. He knew outside the street punks and even some of the middle class dopes were getting deep into heroin. He'd tried that too, but it made him so damn groggy he couldn't even make mealtime, couldn't finish sentences when he tried to talk, and he slept so deeply he thought he'd died. Finally, he'd settled on crank—crystal meth—as a preferred choice because it *really* shook him out of his skin. He didn't want to get sedated or sick or horny. He wanted to fly away, baby. Turn into pure color and rock and roll to pure sound waves. He wanted to jitter and jangle like a windchime in a hurricane. Goddamn right!

He saw everything clearly, moved like there was a train connected to his ass that pushed him into the future.

One out of ten times he might have the shakes so bad he couldn't tie his own shoes. It was nearly worth it. If he got too jazzed, too spaced, he went to Mod Squad and got him to keep an eye on him so the Keys didn't haul him down to isolation or the prison infirmary.

He felt the music from an old Aretha Franklin's blues tune smoothly boring through the back of the leather seat where his head rested. It entered the tangle of his long black hair, sinuously twining between the individual shafts, snaking over the pimply skin of his skull, and then SHA-ZAM! It was in his head, lazily stirring the brain cells into soup, alphabet music soup.

Heddy's voice echoed from a canyon. "You have to do that shit when I'm driving? Crow?"

He couldn't tell her how much her question amused him. He had to do this shit, yes, he did, he had to. When she drove or when she didn't, when the sun shined and when the sky poured, when the earth turned and when it decided to stop. Didn't she know any damn thing? Besides, he didn't want to hear any prissy lectures from a woman who sipped Jim Beam like it was soda water. She stayed half-crocked from morning till night. You couldn't tell unless you got right up in her face and smelled it on her breath. Heddy held her liquor better than any man he'd ever known. Of course, Heddy was a lush, no doubt about it, but did he bug her about it? Fuck no.

He heard whispers and opened his eyes to just a slit. He saw the little girl next to him, whispering to her mother. He reached out one impossibly long arm that ended in a ham-like hand that was much too large to belong to him, and patted her on the top of the head. Good kid, good kid, don't do anything rash, kid, or I have to hurt you.

She couldn't hear his thoughts, of course. And if she could, she'd never make them out from the streams of pale violet and stark red colors that wove like ribbons around, over, and between the tumbling words . . . Good . . . kid . . . Good . . . kid . . . bam, sha-zam, thank you, ma'am, ain't this a lovely world?

* * * * *

I guess I have to tell you the truth. There *is* something funny about how I know what grown-ups are thinking. I said it's just from looking in their eyes, but I'm afraid that's a little story, like a white lie. It's more than that—how I hear thoughts.

Like in the car that first day. After Crow sucked the drug up his nose, I got all confused listening into his thoughts. I don't know how to explain it. . . .

It's like the radio. You know how you're listening to the radio, maybe it's a ballgame? Then some static comes over the station and another station bleeds into it and you hear a song or some commercial for toothpaste or something? That's how it is. I'd never even told my Mama about it until Crow and Heddy took us off. I guess I have to tell you because that's how some of the things happened the way they did.

Mr. Hawkins sat forward in his seat and leaned on the desk. He blew smoke at the ceiling before saying, "We've had to use psychics before."

You believe in them? I asked him.

"Oh, I don't know. They've helped out a time or two."

Well, I don't know what a psychic is, I said. I thought they told fortunes in booths at the fair and I can't tell fortunes. All I know is I get static. Sometimes the static's like thoughts, but I'm not thinking them. So they must come from other people. I never thought much about it because I've always had static in my head, even when I was a baby, as far back as I can remember.

I never told anyone before. I've been afraid to. I know other people can't do this. They'd think I'm crazy or bad moon loony and I don't think I am. I figure maybe it comes from God or something, a way to help protect me maybe. I don't know really. I might know when I'm grown and understand these things better.

Anyway, after Crow took the drug, I started getting his

thoughts all jumbled, mixed up with bright colors and long drawn out music sounds that sounded like guitars holding a note a long time. I knew about how he got drugs in prison and how Heddy wasn't any better, she drank whiskey, kept a pint bottle in her purse, and she took it like medicine. She was a *lush,* he thought, but it didn't bother him.

That's when I slid next to Mama and tried to tell her in a whisper that we were in really bad trouble now. It would have been awful enough if Crow and Heddy were using us and the car to get away and they might let us go soon. But when I found out how much time they spent dreaming inside their heads with drugs and whiskey, I knew we might be stuck with them. They needed help. They couldn't do it without someone to lean on. They weren't getting away with Crow's escape all on their own, they weren't strong enough.

I don't think even Crow and Heddy understood how weak they were without us around. It was like once we were with them, our fear fed them. Not to mention that if they ran into law trouble how better off they were with a policeman and his family for hostages. Cops will do anything for another cop, anything. They knew that. It wasn't unlucky at all, them running into us, the way Heddy said at first. They knew it was lucky, really. We were like solid gold to them.

When I tried to tell Mama in some way she'd understand me, Crow reached out his hand and patted me on the head the way you pat dogs. I heard him say, "Good kid, good kid."

But that's not all. He was thinking, *I don't want to hurt you, just be a good kid.*

He didn't want me to tell Mama what I knew. I even knew about the nasty stuff, the sex stuff he did behind bars so he could keep from being knifed or hit over the head when he was sleeping in his bunk. He used the word "nigger" in his head, a word my Mama told me never ever to say. Anytime I hear someone use that word it makes me want to scrunch up my shoulders and find a corner to go hide in, ashamed I can be in the same room with someone who calls a black person that word. It makes me want to say the same thing my Mama told me. "Skin color is an accident. If you'd been born black would you want white people calling you a name like that? Would you?"

But I knew Crow had been calling them that a long time, probably all his life. He didn't know any better, no one had taught him anything.

I looked at him next to me with his eyes closed and his head against the seat and I knew if I said much about what I knew was in his head to Mama, he'd get really mad. He would hurt me. I'd have to keep most of my thoughts—and Crow's thoughts—to myself. If I talked about it, he'd know.

See, they were both ready to hurt us, but Crow was the one who scared me the most in the beginning. Later, it would be Heddy. It's like the longer we were with them, the truer we could see them, the more we knew about the danger we were in.

He'd seen people hurt in prison and he'd done some of that hurting. He'd been put in Leavenworth for trying to kill a man with a pool stick. He'd gotten mad over a bet and broke the stick over the other man's head, then stuck the broken end into the man's stomach. He pulled it out and started kicking the man in the head. He'd have killed him if some other men hadn't pulled him off.

I know this because during the time we were with them, he bragged about it to my Dad. My Daddy just shook his head and ground his teeth.

"You're nothing but a gutter punk," Daddy said.

"Yeah, like you never busted a guy over the head, you freaking pig liar asshole. I guess you'd like me better if I was one of those psycho killers that jerk off over dead bodies and eat their livers with onions on the side."

Daddy said, "If you think you're better, you're sadly mistaken."

"What I'm thinking I'm mistaken about is not throwing your ass out of this car while Heddy's doing eighty miles an hour." Then Crow laughed to beat the band until Heddy told him to shut up, sit back, and get a grip.

Since escaping, Crow and Heddy had robbed a gas station outside of St. Louis. Crow didn't like the way the gas station attendant looked at Heddy, like he was about to make fun of how half her mouth didn't work right, so he shot him three times.

They hadn't said that on the radio yet because they didn't know it had been Crow. This was something I knew when Crow took the drug. He started sort of reliving it. Playing it over in his head, all of it running fast like a movie going crazy, and I got the static from him.

"That's pretty odd you know about that," Hawkins said, lighting a new cigarette. "It's true, too. The killer was Craig Walker. The man you call Crow. Missouri State police got a make on the car that was identified as being at the scene of the crime. It matched the car they left in the woods near the Long Horn Caverns."

So you believe me, I guess, I said.

It was hard knowing things and not being able to tell my mother or father. Daddy already knew they were really dangerous. He knew all about bad people so they weren't fooling him any. But Mama only knows a little about people like Crow and Heddy. She didn't know how easy it would be for Crow to pull out the gun and kill us for nothing, for looking at him funny or pushing him too far or saying something that bothered him. I was trying to warn her, but I couldn't.

The whole car used to smell like a new car. Even when we drove up to the caverns, it still smelled like new leather and carpet and vinyl. But after Crow and Heddy were in the car, it smelled like putrid stuff . . . old food standing in a refrigerator that's stopped working. Curdled yogurt and green slimy vegetables and meat that's turned gray.

"Mama, roll down the window," I said.

"You're not rolling down the windows," Heddy said, looking at me over her shoulder with a big frown plastered on her face. "I'll turn up the air if you're hot."

"I have to go to the bathroom."

"Wait a while. You can wait."

"For godssake, she's a kid. She has to go to the bathroom," Daddy said.

"She's a big kid, is what she is. She can hold it until we get down the road a ways."

Crow rolled his head and lifted it. He opened his eyes. "Listen to Heddy. Don't give us trouble."

He laid his head back and drifted off, coming down from the nervous strain of the drug high. I didn't ask again. An hour later, Heddy slowed down a couple of miles outside of a town and turned into a dirt road that didn't look like it led anywhere. It wound and curved between thick trees that made a dark forest on each side. She stopped and told me to get out. And Mama too.

Crow woke up and watched, curious. "What's happening?"

"I'm letting them take a piss."

"Do I have to, Mama?" I asked. Because we were outside the car in a ditch now and Heddy told us to squat and pee.

"This is terrible," Mama said to Heddy.

"It's going to be worse if you have to hold it and wet your pants. Now squat!"

Mama took me behind the car bumper and we both went to the bathroom in the road, in the dirt, leaving puddles between our knees. Mama had brought tissues from her purse. She told me not to worry, not to be scared. I couldn't help it. I could hardly go to the bathroom. Heddy started screaming at us and finally I was able to.

I was hoping a car would come down the road and see us squatting there, going to the bathroom like animals in the road. They'd know something was wrong.

But no one came. We got back in the car; Heddy turned around and drove back to the highway.

"No more stopping," Heddy said, once she was on the highway.

"I'm getting hungry," Crow said. He rubbed his skinny stomach and grinned at me like he could get me to smile at him. I didn't.

"Oh, Crow, we can't get anything right now. Let's just try to get out of this fucking state, okay?"

"Sure, okay, baby. But we get into Kansas and I want food."

"My mom lives in Kansas," Heddy said.

"So?" Crow leaned forward until he was just inches from the back of her head. "She a good cook or what?"

Heddy grunted. "Hell no, she's no cook. I lived on oatmeal when I stayed with her."

"Then what's the point? She lives in Kansas, so freaking what?"

"I might go by. Just for a few minutes. I don't think anyone knows where she lives now but me. I need to tell her where I'm going."

"Like she won't tell. That's not too smart, Heddy." Crow leaned back, exasperated.

"You let me worry about what she'd tell."

Heddy turned up the radio and drove. She was like a machine, driving the car. She didn't talk or look at us. From where I sat I could see one side of her face, the side that worked okay. It was as paralyzed and dead as the other side. She might as well have been a wooden Indian.

I wondered what her mother was like, if she was nice like my mom, and decided she probably wasn't. I hoped we didn't have to go there, to her mom's. Suddenly a feeling came over me that Crow was right—it was a dumb idea to go see Heddy's mom. But not because she might tell anything to the police. It was something else about the idea that bothered me and I didn't know what it was. I never figured it out until we got there either.

Crow asked questions of Daddy and Mama, but when they didn't say much, he gave up, put his head back, and fell asleep again, his drug high winding down.

That's how our first day went. We were hostages heading into Kansas and we might get to meet Heddy's mother. The vacation was over.

When Heddy had put the Missouri-Kansas state line fifty miles behind her, she said to Jay, "How much money do you have?"

"A couple of hundred."

"Give Crow your wallet."

She watched him carefully as he withdrew his wallet from his back pocket and handed it over the back seat.

"How much he got?" she asked.

"Two-forty."

"Credit cards?"

"A couple. Visa and MasterCard. Oh, and there's a Sears card too." He laughed. "We got us a real bunch of middle class citizens here."

"Keep the cash and cards. He can't do much if he's got no money on him. I'm going to find a motel," Heddy said, slowing for a town speed limit sign. "Then I can get something for us to eat while you watch them in the room."

"Sounds like a plan," Crow said.

Jay glanced at Crow. "Why don't you let us go? You're over the state line now. You've got the car. Take my money, the credit cards. Just let us out somewhere."

"Heddy, he's talking to me. Tell him not to talk to me."

"Shut up," she said, craning her head forward over the wheel to check out motel signs.

"What's the point of keeping us?"

"He's talking again. You hear him?"

Heddy frowned at the passenger sitting next to her. "We'll let you go when we get good and ready to let you go. If you keep yapping, Crow's gonna lose his cool and hit you again. I think you should shut up when I tell you to shut up. That's just my friendly advice, though, you do what you got to do."

Jay straightened in his seat, face forward.

Heddy spied a vacancy sign in front of a small rundown motel where the rooms were separate cabins arranged around a large semi-circle grassy drive. She turned in, parked out of sight of the office, and told Crow to watch them. He handed the cash from Jay's wallet over the seat to her before she exited the Riviera.

It was easy getting the room farthest from the office. Most of the cabins were empty.

"The freeway took away all our business," the old man at the counter said in a pitiful voice. "The whole town's been dying."

Heddy didn't comment and she didn't smile. She never smiled at strangers who would look at her funny because half her mouth wouldn't move. Better they thought her sullen. She just took the key and left the office. Back in the car, she drove them to the cabin and helped Crow herd the family inside and out of sight.

"Now you keep an eye on the Brady Bunch while I go find something for us to eat."

Crow grabbed her from behind and nuzzled her neck. He had his gun out and the kid right at his side. Heddy laughed and pulled away. "Don't take your eyes off them. I'll bring back rope so we can tie them up later."

"Awright! Sounds kinky!"

Heddy almost smiled, but it didn't quite reach her mouth.

With Heddy gone, the room began to impress itself on the people remaining in the shabby room. The family cowered and shivered as if from the frigid air that blew from the noisy window unit. Crow cursed at what a dump the place was before ripping off a threadbare chenille cover from one of the two double beds. The whooping sound of the cover coming loose from the mattress and the wheezing air conditioner were the only sounds. "I hate shitty places like this. They probably got bedbugs."

Jay stood quietly watching from in front of a built-in desk connected to one wall. It was obvious to look at his face that he was desperately working out some kind of escape plan to put into force.

Emily backed up to the room's window that looked out over the gravel courtyard fronting the cabin. She looked more scared than she had at any time since the abduction.

Carrie sat down wearily on the mattress and stared at the floor, her hands limp on the bed at her sides.

Jay said, "You don't have to tie us up later. We're not going to do anything."

"Don't tell me what I don't have to do. Heddy's right, she's always right. I'm not about to sit here all night with a gun on all three of you."

"We won't give you any trouble. Haven't we cooperated so far?"

"I'm ignoring you, jerk-off."

Jay hesitated. "I don't understand why you want to keep us around."

Crow, as he had done before, lashed out without warning, striking Jay, who stood a few inches taller, across the cheek with the gun's barrel. It caused the larger man to stagger and bump into the desk. He reached out for the phone in order to lift it as a weapon, but Crow moved in quickly, burying the gun in Jay's stomach.

"You really want to crawl outta here holding your guts?"

Jay's fingers loosened on the phone, his hand moved away and finally dropped to his side. The blow to his face this time didn't break the skin so there was no blood, but a red mark three inches long rose from his chin to his eye. Now his entire face had been battered. His left eye was hardly a slit from the first time he'd been hit in the car.

"Please, can I talk to you?" Carrie asked in a tremulous voice.

"Pretty woman like you? Want to beg me? Want to

barter, lady? With your own kid watching?"

Color rose in Carrie's face. "We haven't done anything to warrant your behavior," she said in a schoolmistress tone of voice. "My husband's right. There's no point in keeping us hostage. We're not going to be able to help you."

"Hey, come over here, kid. Mom and Pop don't seem to get it."

Emily slowly crossed the room.

"Leave her alone. I told you that already. We're doing what you want." Carrie sounded stronger and her eyes flashed angrily.

Crow reached out and hugged the girl to his leg. He kept the gun at his waist level, pointed to the child's head. "Remember this kid's mine. She goes first if either one of you try to get smart with me."

Before Heddy returned with food, the Anderson family members were subdued. Jay and Carrie lay on one bed on their sides facing the door. Emily sat upright in the chair in the corner by the window. Her hands lay in her lap and her ankles dangled off the chair seat edge.

Heddy came in with two boxes of pizza and a bag containing two cold liters of Pepsi. "Good job!" she said, seeing the family so motionless and silent.

Crow turned down the volume on the television. "God, I could eat one of those pizzas whole, all by myself."

To the family's horror, after the pizza had been shared and eaten, Heddy and Crow started discussing leaving the two adults tied to trees in a wooded area outside of town and taking the kid with them the next day.

Carrie, too frightened of the plan to be afraid for her own welfare, protested vehemently. "Let us all go," she pleaded. "What you're talking about is crazy."

"She's kind of cute, huh?" Crow asked Heddy. "Listen,

lady, we might just keep you all too. Don't butt in."

"You could get a boner for her? I think she's kind of fat."

Crow shrugged.

"On the other hand, her husband's not bad looking . . ."

"You want him? Take him. It might be fun seeing a guy get it from a woman."

"Oh God," Carrie said, turning her face into the pillow. "You are sick people."

"You're a couple of real animals, you know that?" Jay said. "You've got the morals of weasels."

"Take the girl into the bathroom and let her sit on the floor a while," Heddy said to Crow. "Her Daddy needs a lesson in humility from a weasel."

* * * * *

That night when Heddy found a room, things got really awful. They took me into the bathroom and set me against the tub on the floor. I heard everything. The sounds of someone slapping someone. The bed noise, creaking and shaking. There was a lot of laughing and my Mama was crying for a while, but I think they must have put a gag in her mouth because I didn't hear her later. Daddy said stuff to them, really mean stuff, but they hit him again—I heard him grunt in pain—and he didn't say another word the whole time.

I could have tried to listen in to one of their thoughts, but I was afraid to. I didn't want to really know what was happening. I could tell it was pretty awful.

I don't know if Heddy . . . did things . . . with my Daddy, but whatever they did that night it changed everything.

I was brought out late, maybe after midnight, and they made me a place on the floor with a pillow and a sheet over me. My hands and feet were tied, but I slept a little. I tried to lift my head to see Mama and Daddy, but I couldn't see over the mattress. After a while I heard Crow snoring, but I never knew if Heddy slept or not. The TV was on all night, turned down low. Maybe she was watching it. I couldn't see it from the floor, but I listened for a long time, thinking maybe the news would come on and say they were about to find Crow and Heddy. I fell asleep during a commercial show about an exercise machine. I never did hear any news.

The next morning after Heddy brought us donuts and coffee, we were untied and told to go to the bathroom, we were leaving and we weren't stopping again for a long time. Heddy said she didn't want to stop until she got to her mom's house.

Daddy and Mama looked so different. It was like Daddy's mind had slipped over the edge to peek at something gross he'd never seen before and couldn't figure out once he did see it. He wasn't all there. I looked at him, trying to see into his mind, but he was closed off, sealed in. His eyes darted like little lizards as he stared at the floor. He hardly ever looked up except to see where he was going. He wouldn't look at me. Or Mama. No one.

Mama just looked sad, the way she used to after her and Daddy had had a fight and he'd hit her. She wouldn't look at me either.

Crow and Heddy acted like they were having a party. It

was like Halloween, but the monsters weren't masked; they were real.

I guess they'd given up the idea of leaving my parents behind and taking just me. We all got into the car and Heddy drove again across the state of Kansas on small two-lane highways that went through lots of little towns out in the middle of nowhere.

They gave us hotdogs from a Dairy Queen for lunch. Heddy said she loved hotdogs better than anything. After that, we had them at least once a day.

I can't stand hotdogs now.

After Jay was moved from the bed where his wife lay and pushed down on the other bed, Heddy got Crow to help her take down his pants until they were tangled around his tied ankles.

She unbuttoned his shirt and spread it open to reveal a bare hairless chest. She crawled on top of him and whispered in his ear. "Crow really will kill your kid, you know. If you don't play along with us, you're all going to be dead. Do you believe me?"

Jay twisted his face from her. He refused to answer.

Heddy reached down and took his penis into her hand. She looked over at the other bed to see if Carrie was watching. She wasn't. Her eyes were squeezed closed. She looked like she was constipated.

Crow kneeled next to the bed, his eyes glittering with

lust. She'd take care of him in a few minutes. She smiled her half smile at him and he grinned back at her like a crazy, wild baboon with the hots.

She wriggled over Jay's body, pressing her naked flesh against his chest. She lifted herself a little and dragged her right nipple over his left one. She felt him shudder uncontrollably. He turned his face to her and stared into her eyes. She stared back, rubbing against him harder. She teased his cock and cupped his balls in her hand. She tightened her grip slowly until he tensed.

"If this takes a while, that's all right. I don't mind waiting. I got all night." She turned her head to Crow. "Isn't that right, Crow? You mind waiting?"

He shook his head, mesmerized by Heddy's sexual extravagance. They had done this before, shared others, but never someone who didn't want to play.

"Your wife a good lay?" she asked Jay. "I bet she's not. I bet she's dull as dishwater. I bet she lies there like a fucking stone. Am I right? You're sick of her, tell me how sick of her you are. Tell me how often you've gone out on her and fucked her friends.

"You think I'm pretty? Hmmm?"

Heddy ran her tongue into his ear and down his neck. She left a wet trail across one nipple, flicking her tongue over his abdomen, pausing at his navel. She finally moved down and took him into her mouth.

"What a good girl you are," Crow piped excitedly. He reached over and took hold of the globes of her ass and squeezed.

Jay was not the most useful partner she'd ever encountered, but Heddy managed to get him hard and ride him toward one strong orgasm before he bucked her off, grunting around the gag in his mouth, his penis shriveling even before it slipped from her wetness.

Heddy rolled to the edge of the bed into Crow's arms and let him spread her on the floor between the two beds. He was so excited he could hardly wait. He got inside her and was pumping like a locomotive before she could draw a good breath. If she had been the laughing sort, she would have burst into gay, unbridled laughter at how eager he was to spend himself where another man hadn't been able.

It was a long time before they were satiated and remembered the girl in the bathroom, sitting on the floor waiting for someone to come get her.

While Crow pulled up and buckled Jay's trousers, Heddy led the girl into the room and placed her on a pillow on the floor at the end of her bed. She covered her with a sheet and crawled into the bed between Jay and Crow to sleep.

As far as she knew the woman in the other bed never opened her eyes all night. Hell, if she couldn't get laid, she might as well sleep so maybe she'd have a wet dream, poor old fat thing.

Heddy laughed to herself while the two men on each side of her fell into deep sleeps and Crow began to snore.

She'd changed her mind about leaving the parents and taking the kid. It was way too much fun having everyone along. She hadn't had so much fun in ages, goddamn if she had. Also, what if they got caught? If they had hostages along, they might have a chance to bargain their way out.

And to tell the truth, Jay had a bigger cock than Crow. The guy was hung like King Kong, for crying out loud. If he'd only start using it, what a good time she could have.

Besides, he smelled good when he worked up a sweat. Not like Crow, who most often started stinking like a homeless tramp when he got a lather up. Even if she did like a man's sweaty scent, there happened to be some she liked more than others.

* * * * *

Frank Hawkins settled back in the old wood secretary's chair behind the desk when the girl began to tell him about the first night the family spent with their abductors. He realized (and thought the girl did too) that Heddy had had sex with Jay Anderson while his daughter was locked in a bathroom.

It made Frank crawl with the creeps. During their sessions, Jay had admitted to playing around on his wife. Frank tried to gently point out that it was his guilt over extra-marital affairs that helped fuel his anger he eventually took out at home on his family. Jay didn't buy that. Too painful to accept all responsibility, of course. Much easier to deny culpability.

Jay never came right out and said he talked female law-breakers into having sex with him in exchange for tearing up a traffic violation ticket or for reducing charges, but Frank suspected he misused his authority in that manner too. If he had ever admitted it outright, of course Frank would have had no alternative but to follow procedure and report it to the sheriff, getting Jay removed or suspended.

The most liability Jay did admit to was that he frequently cheated on his wife. How and with whom was something he wasn't ready to discuss.

Frank remembered a few things Jay had said regarding his sex life. For one thing he had strong fantasies. Now it was Hawkins' experience that a good fantasy life was nothing to be worried about and in most instances it indicated good mental health, but Jay obsessed on the sexual fantasies to an extreme degree. Most of his waking time was spent thinking about them.

Jay had said once, "You know what I wish I could get in this country? A basket fuck."

"I'm sorry, what's that again?" Frank had been taking notes, most of it doodling, drawing Popeye with his corncob pipe, and he hadn't been as attentive as he might have been. Had he heard correctly?

"You never heard of a basket fuck? I knew a guy, patrolman partner in Charlotte when I worked down here, had been in the Navy. He told me about getting this thing in Japan while on shore leave. How it works is they got the guy down on a pallet, giving him a massage. One girl is sitting naked in a basket with a hole in the bottom. Two girls get the client hard and salved or lotioned up and they position the girl right on top of him. There's a pulley system holding the basket so all the other two have to do is lift and lower it on the guy. When he's ready to climax, one of the girls gives the basket a twirl. I think about that all the time. But where are you going to find three girls willing to set it up? This is America, after all."

Frank hummed a little to show he was listening, but made no judgmental call on the fantasy. A lot of guys liked an exotic bit of sex now and then, no big deal. But as their sessions wore on, Frank heard other fantasies that were even more unusual than the Japanese basket trick. It seemed that Jay had an active sex drive and an overactive imagination. If he could imagine it, he wanted it.

Heddy's appeal had something to do with all that. There had been men who would follow a woman like her across the face of the planet. Maybe Jay had been one of them.

Frank focused on the little girl and listened as she returned to her story. There was so much missing from the puzzle of the Anderson abduction. Only the kid knew the details. If he was to understand, he had to listen closely.

* * * * *

After the escape from Leavenworth, planned and executed with the help of seven other inmates, only six of whom, including Crow, actually made it away from the prison before getting nabbed, Crow split from his fellow escapees. He met Heddy where she waited for him in a rusty-pancled, smoke-belching Dodge Dart. The state police were immediately contacted when the breakout occurred and swarms of cops spread out in all four directions trying to capture the cons before the six o'clock news teams got hold of it to take it national.

They did not succeed. Within ten hours they had only corralled one of the escapees. Crow and the others had scattered into the four winds, free!

With that many convicts on the lam, Heddy told him his chances of getting away were increased. It had been her idea, months before on a visit to him, that he bring in several others on the plan. They acted as camouflage and sucker bait for one another. The cops were running around like chickens with their heads cut off trying to track them all down.

Heddy said this should give them time to make a quick trip to St. Louis where she'd been living. There was a drug lab there, a big one, a really hot lab. She found this out from the crowd she ran with while he was locked up those four years. A boyfriend of a girlfriend (she claimed, though Crow figured the boyfriend was someone she was screwing) worked there, an amateur chemist, an assistant, if you will. He was the one who mentioned the back room during some unguarded moment. (In the sack with Heddy, no doubt.) It all came gushing out of him like a flash flood, she said. The money. The tables stacked with bills. It seemed that not only were the chemicals on the premises, but in a back room of the house they kept the haul from the sales until it got parceled out and moved out of the house. "You know," the guy told Heddy, "that two fifty-five gallon drums of common chemicals can make nine *billion* dollars worth of methadexadrine?"

"You got a billion dollars in that house? Or nine billion?"

"Hell, no, they don't have that much made all at once and it takes time to make the deals to off-load that much crystal—it gets distributed all over the fucking Midwest— but still, there's plenty of green in the back. Don't ever breathe a word of this, though." He began licking his lips nervously and looking around him as if he thought invisible spies watched and listened. "They find out I told you, they'd take off my balls with a pipe cutter."

He sported dreadlocks and a tattoo that crept from his chest up around his collarbone to circle his scrawny neck. Heddy said it might have been a snake. Or a lizard. Or it could even have been a tree root. It was ugly anyway, nothing like the small black spider tattoo of her own that graced the lower portion of one buttock, or the tiny perfect sword tattoo she'd asked to be positioned over her right breast so that the tip pointed to her heart. She didn't care what the goofy lab man's tattoo was. She just cared about the information.

Pretending she didn't know about his tattoo convinced Crow she'd bedded him. Why go into that kind of song and dance if she hadn't? Not that he cared. He didn't care. Was she supposed to swear off sex for four years while he was in the joint? He sure as hell hadn't, had he? And Heddy was a firecracker. She liked fucking almost as much as whiskey.

They'd need money like that, like what was on those tables in the back room of the lab, she'd told Crow. They needed it to keep him out, to insure his freedom. Hell, they wouldn't have had to rob the convenience store on the way if she could have rounded up some cash to take them across state. But she couldn't hit the lab house alone. No fucking way.

Heddy wasn't scared of the lab's owners after they ripped it off; she just couldn't pull the job alone. She was no more afraid of the gangs running the lab than she was afraid of the law, she said, and Crow knew she had never been scared of the law. She'd broken it enough on misdemeanor and a few felony charges that it had lost all fear for her. They could only kill her once, that's what she always said.

The lab robbery didn't make the news, of course. Thieves stealing from thieves didn't interest Mr. and Mrs. Bobby John Smith while they got up supper for their five screaming kids. The deaths were hushed up. Bodies must have been trucked down to the river and dropped in wearing necklaces of concrete blocks during the dead of night.

Knocking over the lab house had been one chilly business. Without Heddy's gifted idea of having them lie down on the floor all in a line with their hands positioned above their heads, he never could have been able to shoot six big muscle-bound gorillas fast enough to save his head from being ripped right off his shoulders.

With them on their bellies, though, and the duct tape Heddy wrapped around their wrists, it was a duck shoot. He simply walked down the line in front of them, put the gun to their heads, and good-bye, lowlife lab goon. It wasn't like they didn't know the risks in the lifestyle they'd chosen.

He had some of the money in his leather purse he always kept by his side. Heddy had more of it in *her purse,* the one where she carried her whiskey bottle and a change of clothes. And there was more. They hadn't even tried to count it, though it was no billion dollars, he knew that much. Eighteen thick rubber-bound stacks of wrinkled, unmarked fifties and hundreds. That's what they had. At least, that's what Heddy thought they had. Enough.

"Where do we go with this?" he'd asked her after they'd left St. Louis and just before they noticed they had a patrol car tailing them—the event that pushed them toward the Long Horn Caverns.

"Anywhere your little black heart pleases," she'd said, smiling her crooked smile.

That's what he liked about Heddy. She knew him and still loved him enough to break him out. He wasn't always sure he knew her so well. Like the lab house thing. That was pretty risky, slipping them in the back door, taking the place unaware that way.

The guy with the tattoo wasn't there, must not have been his shift. Lucky bastard. His absence saved him from winding up with the other corpses found bound and headshot in the living room of the house on Prairie Avenue.

Minutes before they saw the cop tail, Crow leaned over

and gave Heddy a long kiss. "We're rich!" he'd said.

Heddy brought her hand up to cover her mouth as she smiled. She had told him early on her mouth didn't work right from an open-handed hit she took from her stepfather when she was thirteen. Crow crooned sweet love noises against that paralyzed side of her lips when she told him and promised to kill any motherfucker ever raised a hand to her again. Kill him deader than dead. Kill him two times.

That's why—the money in his bag, his freedom from Leavenworth, and the promise of Heddy's sweet frozen lips—when she changed her mind about letting the mother and father go, Crow said okay, sure, I don't care, baby, whatever you say.

Now he sat in the back seat, Heddy driving at all the right speed limits while they rolled through small Kansas cow towns, and he tried to get to know the woman in the back seat with him. She was really too old for him, hell, she had to be thirty if she was a day, what with a kid ten years old, but if Heddy was going to get some of Jay, he definitely was going to get some of Carrie. She wasn't fat, like Heddy made out. She was plumpish and he liked that.

He wondered a lot about her breasts and how big they were when loosened from the bra he could tell she wore beneath her cool white blouse. Her arms looked ripe and firm. Her legs, bare in the tan walking shorts she wore, were heavy, but smooth and creamy like mocha almond coffee you can get in the Stop 'n Robs.

"What grade do you teach?" he asked.

She turned her head from the window, her eyes glazed. "Me?"

"Yeah you. You're a schoolteacher, right?"

"I teach fifth grade."

"Where'd you get that bruise on your arm?" He reached

over and brushed his fingers lightly across a mark the size of a baby's fist. It looked over a week old, fading away now, the purple turning the sick yellow of an overripe banana.

Her eyes darted to the back of Jay's head and then down to her hands folded tightly in her lap.

"She doesn't want to talk to you," the little girl said.

"She doesn't want to talk about the bruise, you mean. Hey, Jay! You go around banging on your ole lady, don't you? Nice guy like you, I never would have guessed. Big strong cop. Not enough to beat on the guy in the street, is that it? You got to knock your woman around too."

Jay turned in the front seat. "I don't know what you're talking about."

"Like hell you fucking don't know what I'm talking about."

"Do we have to talk?" Carrie asked, turning again to the window. "I don't want to talk about it."

"You like your daddy?" Crow asked the little girl.

She nodded her head.

"Even though he beats up your mom? You really like him, huh?"

He could see the confusion in the girl's eyes. "It's okay. I always liked my folks too, even though they didn't deserve it. That's how it is for kids." He leaned forward and said to Heddy, "Tell them what happened to your mouth."

"Let it go, Crow. I don't wanna talk about it no more than she does."

He settled back. "Her dad—her step-dad—punched her. That's what happened. Messed up the nerves or something in her face. Tell them what you did, Heddy, go on."

"I stuck a butter knife through his ribs. When he got out of the hospital he never hit me again."

"There," Crow said. "That's what you do to guys knock

59

around their women and their kids. You stick 'em. You fuck 'em up good with butter knives!" Then he laughed, slapping his knee, until the little girl interrupted him by putting her hand on his arm.

"Why don't you get another car?" she asked in a small, quiet voice. "There must be lots of other cars you can get."

Crow turned to her, but his gaze shifted to Carrie. The woman hovered like a wounded butterfly pressed against the window glass. "Face it, kid. We're your world for as long as Heddy says we are."

She let his arm go, giving up. He looked at Carrie, staring at the bra straps through her white shirt, and wondered why she hadn't ever taken a knife or a club or a gun to her slap-happy cop husband.

She wasn't anything like Heddy. Heddy was great, she was smart, she got him free, but she was a cheap perfume imitation of a name brand, she was bikini underwear from the Wal-Mart, she was ham hocks and beans. Carrie was prize and prime and almost girlish in her innocence.

Oh yeah, he was gonna have her. Oh yeah.

Crow wanted to get in a bed with my Mama. I didn't even have to listen in to his thoughts to know it. You could see it in his face when he looked at her.

I know about sex. They teach us in school. Men and women get in a bed together and they have parts that fit. The man has a penis and the woman has a vagina. When they're in love, they stick them together. That's how babies get made. Sometimes they kiss, too, with their tongues out. I've seen it in the movies, but that looks so nasty I can't stand it. I wouldn't want nobody's spit in *my* mouth.

But Crow didn't love my Mama and he wasn't thinking about kissing. He just wanted to do the sex thing in a bed with her.

I looked at the back of Heddy's head and wondered what she'd do if Crow bothered my Mama. She might get jealous and kill them!

Then I looked at Mama staring out the window and knew she had no idea what was ahead of her if we didn't get away from Crow and Heddy. She didn't know she was going to have to do . . . stuff . . . with someone she didn't know, someone who scared her.

I tried to think what to do. Crow kept his gun and my Daddy's gun in his purse. If I could ever get my hand in there without him seeing me . . .

But he kept it too close. He hugged it like you hug a baby doll. It was a fat purse and it had to have all kinds of stuff in it besides the guns and the tinfoil squares of drugs and the Wrigley's gum. I'd never get it away from him. He might be skinny, but he was real strong. When he picked me up from the bathroom floor it was like he had picked up a bag of apples. He had all these muscles in his arms from being in prison and working out, he said.

"Where we going now?" Crow asked of Heddy once he got his fill of staring at Mama.

"I'm going to head south soon," she said. "Soon as we make that quick stop at my mom's."

"I wish we didn't have to make that stop. I've been dreaming of Mexico. I really did check out some books teaching Spanish like you said, Heddy, but I didn't get far with them. About all I picked up from the Chicanos in Leavenworth was *frijoles* and *puta*." He laughed. "Yeah, we be going down into sunshine country."

"You're heading for Mexico. Why can't you let us go?" Daddy asked. It was the first thing he'd said all morning.

"Because I like you," she said, giving him one of her lopsided grins. "Didn't I prove that last night?"

"People we know are going to report we haven't called in. They'll tell the police we were at the Long Horn Caverns. They'll put it together and know you're in our car."

"Bullshit. You hear that bullshit, Crow? Is that the biggest bullshit you ever heard or what?"

"Yeah, I hear the motherfucker. What if he's right?"

"He's making it all up. They didn't call anyone when they were at the caverns. That was a tourist stop thing, spur of the moment. No one knows they went there."

"That right, cop? You're trying to fool us? I could hurt you for that."

Then something crazy happened. Daddy grabbed the wheel and hauled it hard to his side of the car. Crow was slammed against the car door and me and Mama fell over on him. Heddy was screaming like some kind of cat, real high scary sounds. The car ran off the road and jumped a ditch. We hit a barbed wire fence, knocking it flat. We went bumping and careening before Heddy stomped the brakes and we slid around in the middle of a cow pasture.

Daddy was out of the car and running hard as he could back toward the highway. It was a two-lane road and there weren't many cars. One went by now and then, but not right when he was running toward it.

Crow fumbled open the back door and fell out onto his shoulder yelping. He scrambled up and pulled out his gun. He aimed it and shot at Daddy.

I was trying to get out of the car too, but Mama held me fast by the back of my shirt. I saw Daddy drop. There was the shot and then he dropped to the ground. I thought he'd been killed.

"Daddy!"

Heddy was out of the car by then, taking the keys. Crow and Heddy ran toward Daddy, both of them waving guns and I thought I was going to faint. Everything started getting black around the edges, like the world was squeezing in toward the center where Daddy lay.

I saw him sit up. I saw his grim face with dirt on it. I saw Crow reach him first and shout something. Then Heddy got there and she leaped right onto Daddy, knocking him to the ground again. She was yelling and clawing at his face while he tried to keep her off him.

The eerie thing was what happened next. Crow started laughing. It was this wild laugh that made the black and white spotted cattle move across the field away from us like we were way too alien for their company. He laughed so hard, he doubled over and held his stomach, he laughed so hard.

Then I knew Daddy wasn't shot and he wasn't dead. He'd hit the ground to keep from being shot in the back. And Crow was laughing at how Heddy was trying to claw Daddy's eyes out. He thought it so funny it almost killed him.

I turned to Mama quick and said, "Mama, Crow wants to take you to bed."

Her eyes got really round and she said, "Emily, how do you know something like that?" It sounded like she very much disapproved of me saying it.

"I . . . I can't tell you, but that's what he wants. He's going to do it too and if he does, Daddy's going to try to stop him and he'll get hurt. He may get shot."

"How do you know these things, Emily? I have to know how you know."

"I . . . I hear stuff. I hear what people think."

Mama stared at me like I had grown horns in the top of my head. "I mean it, Mama. I've always been able to do it. It's real weird, but I'm not lying. Like right now, I know you're thinking, 'She can't do that. No one can do that. That's telepathy! There's no such thing!' "

Mama's mouth dropped open. "You *can* read minds! Oh my God."

"You have to believe me. Crow's going to do something to you and if he does, everything's going to go bad, real bad."

"C'mon," she said, "let's run." She grabbed my hand and pulled me out the other side of the car.

It was like Crow read my mind too because he stopped laughing all of a sudden and turned around. He saw us beginning our sprint across the field, Mama pulling me along with her by the hand. He shot at us and just like Daddy, we stopped and we squatted down. I thought I'd heard the whiz of the bullet as it passed us by in the air, but that was imagination, I'm sure. You don't really hear bullets whiz through the air, that's for cartoons.

Crow yelled, "Get your asses back in the car!"

Mama was crying, no noise, and just fat tears rolling down her face when we stood up and started for the car. I told her, "Mama, you can't fight them. If you and Daddy fight them, they're going to kill you."

"I know," she said.

"I'll think of a way to help us," I said.

"Oh, baby, oh Emily, you're just a little girl," she said, tears choking her.

"I mean it, Mama. I'll think of a way. Didn't I help you sometimes when Daddy was bad? I found a way of letting you know he was coming home mad. Just don't fight them."

I'd led Daddy off into other avenues of thought sometimes when he started getting mad. I'd ask for help with my schoolwork or say there was a phone call for Mama—anything to break his attention to doing harm to my mother. Most of the time it worked. I knew how to get a grown-up's attention off the track and onto something else.

Daddy was back at the car with Crow and Heddy. Now Crow was angry. He was so mad it looked like a black cloud had descended over his head. Laughing hadn't helped him any. He pushed Daddy back into the car and slammed the car door so hard it sounded like a thunderclap.

He got into the back seat with us and shook his head as if he were disappointed. He said, "Run off again, and your kid gets a bullet in the back, Carrie."

"Don't hurt her," Mama said. "It was my fault."

"Of course it was your fault!"

"It was this motherfucker's fault," Heddy said, putting the car into gear and turning it around slowly in the low grass of the field.

Daddy just sat there. Crow said to him, leaning over the seat, "You try that shit again and I don't shoot over your head next time. You could have killed us all, a stunt like that. Who do you think you are, Sly Stallone?"

"I'm bigger than him."

"The hell you are!" Crow took his fist and knocked Daddy in the back of the head. "You're bigger'n me too, but I've got the gun, you fucking pig!"

"You keep hitting me and we're going to go around, bud."

"What'd you say? Pull over, Heddy!"

"He's jerking you around. Shut up, Jay. You've done enough today. Jay, you grab this wheel again and I'll

65

fucking kill you myself." Heddy drove through the ditch and onto the highway again, the back bumper dragging the ground as it cleared the ditch. A car or two had passed, but no one had noticed the commotion in the field.

"You want to go around with me," Crow said, in a different voice, a low growl of a voice, "and I'll take your balls for a necklace. Don't mistake me for one of your small town candy-ass pussies you put your chokeholds on and beat senseless with a nightstick. You underestimate me and you'll find yourself in a grave, friend."

"Listen to him," Heddy said. "He's not lying to you."

"I'd like to take my chances," Jay said.

"No. You wouldn't." Again Crow bopped him in the back of the head with a closed fist. "And if you don't shut up, I'm going to make Heddy pull down some backwoods road so I can put a bullet between your macho-man eyes."

"Daddy, don't," I said, getting really scared.

"Jay, please," Mama said, sighing so hard it filled the whole car.

Jay nodded as if to say, Okay. Okay, for now. Okay, but I'm going to take the little creep down when I get the chance, just you wait and see.

* * * * *

Heddy knew if they headed south for the border from St. Louis, they would have been caught on the road right away. It's where they would be expected to go from the Long Horn Caverns.

66

Driving into the state of Kansas was to throw off the tails and to find a circuitous route down south. It was also a way to get to say goodbye to her mother. She didn't love her. Well, she guessed she did, in a way, but the woman was her entire family, the only one she had, and if she was going to leave the country, she had to say *something* to the only family she knew.

It took longer, going west then south, but it was the only way to stay away from the cops. By now they must have plastered Crow's image all over the papers and the television news.

"Crow, tonight you have to change your looks."

She was driving south across the state now and bored with the flat land, the vistas of green summer fields. She had no idea what was growing there. The closest she'd ever been to a farm was the St. Louis zoo.

"Why's that, baby?" Crow asked. He had snorted another hit of crank. He sounded like a kid on a drunk. It made her want to reach into her purse and take a sip of Jim Beam. But she never did that in front of people. She'd do it when she could stop for gas and go alone into the bathroom. And she'd take more than a sip, by God. All her nerve ends screamed for the bitter fire of whiskey.

"People know what you look like by now. Some store clerk or gas station jockey's gonna make you."

"I don't wanna cut my hair," he said.

She glanced in the rearview mirror at him. Eyes dancing, those heavily lashed black eyes. His skin so white it was almost blinding. Black beard stubble on his cheeks. And his hair, wavy and long and black as night. She liked it a lot, long hair was her thing, but on Crow it had to go.

"Doesn't matter what you want. We have to shave your head."

"What?" He came up in the back seat, eyes menacing now. "I said I ain't cutting my hair."

"Yes, you are." She would brook no argument on this. With his head shaved, he would look completely different. And she had to get those earrings out of his ears.

"Heddy, I know you're trying to help, but I'm telling you right now, the hair's staying."

She grinned at the road ahead. He'd do what she said. He knew he wasn't going to make it without her. He would still be in Leavenworth if it weren't for her. She was the brain and much as he might protest, he listened in the end.

She saw a Texaco station and slowed. "I've got to get gas and take a piss. You watch them," she said to Crow.

"I need to go to the bathroom too," the little girl said.

"After me," Heddy told her. "You just sit there quietly and don't aggravate Crow until I get back."

She parked by the pump and got out of the car. She walked directly to the side of the service station building to the ladies' room. Inside, she locked the door. She found the pint bottle of Jim Beam and twisted off the cap. The first swallow was harsh and she winced. The second swallow was smooth as drinking warm buttered rum coffee. She held up the pint and eyed it. Needed a new one tonight. She'd go out to buy an electric razor to shave Crow and get herself a new bottle. Maybe two.

She slipped the pint into her purse, relieved herself, and stood in front of the mirror on the wall over the sink, staring at her image. The whiskey worked wonders in only minutes. She felt more herself, more real. When she got the jitters between drinks, she thought she might be about to fly apart, break up into jigsaw puzzle pieces no one could put together again. All her insides went into spasm. She got stomach cramps and a burning in her esophagus. Her mind started tripping, going in several directions at once. Nattering at her about this and about that until she thought she might go insane.

She didn't know why Crow favored speed. That stuff warped you right up into a frenzy. He was always picking at stuff, fiddling with his purse, combing his hands through his hair, tapping out drumbeats with his fingertips, jiggling around on the balls of his feet. Some days he went without food, no appetite at all, and when he crashed he was so depressed he was suicidal.

Right now, though, she wasn't about to worry about Crow. With the liquor racing through her system, she felt wonderfully whole. She never smiled at herself in mirrors. The dead half of her mouth could make her so angry she'd been known to shatter mirrors with her fist. But she stared into her own eyes and communicated with the smart, strong, silently watching person there.

We'll make it. We'll make it out alive. We'll be so rich, we'll party every day and every night. Forever. I'll have a maid and a cook and a fine car, one even better than that Riviera. . . .

Someone tapped on the bathroom door. She turned to it and clicked over the lock. If it was that kid, she'd slap her little face until her eyes rolled.

She pulled open the door, ready to go into action. It wasn't the girl standing outside waiting. It was a man. A man who knew her.

"We just want the money back," he said. "You know you shouldn't have done that."

"Rory," she whispered, surprised to see the tattooed loverboy who told her about the money in the lab house. He wore a suit, a plaid shirt open at the collar, no tie. He looked like a used car salesman. Who had dressed him, his mom? Who had sent him? Heddy blinked, trying to get a handle on what he'd just said.

"They sent you? You've followed us?" she asked.

"Heddy, you don't rob St. Louis. I've been following you for two days. I don't know what you and the con are up to with the people in that car, but if you'll just give me the money, you can go on your way, I'll forget all about it. They said they'd even write off the murders and that's pretty unusual, especially since it took a large crew to dispose of the bodies."

While he was talking, Heddy had slipped her hand into the purse and wrapped her fingers around the little .25 caliber automatic she carried there. No matter what Rory promised, she knew he lied.

She lifted the gun into position inside the purse slowly, aiming it at his gut. "Look," she said. "I want you to back off. I want you to go over to your car and haul ass. You need to forget you ever caught up with us. It's that simple. And it's the only warning I'm going to give you."

He gave her a fake sad smile. "Can't do it, babe. I've been sent to collect."

She pulled the trigger twice in rapid succession without giving herself time to think. The sounds were like little pithy backfires from a car. She hoped no one came running around the side of the building and turned this into real trouble.

Rory's eyes registered shock first and then they held nothing. Before he ever fell to the ground, he was dead. She'd gotten him right in the chest where his heart should have been. She didn't think she'd ever made such a lucky shot as that before. It was like fortune was with her.

Heddy stepped over him, blocking the dead look on his face from her mind, and hurried around the building. Her purse was torn and she had to carry it in her arms to keep the contents from falling out. She got into the Riviera, switched on the ignition, and pulled from the pump, the back tires giving a little squeal.

Crow said, "I thought you were getting gas."

The little girl said, "I had to go to the bathroom!"

Heddy shook now. She had to grip the steering wheel hard. She drove the speed limit, watching in her mirrors for anyone following. She hoped Rory had come alone.

"Crow, there was someone back there."

"Who?"

"Someone from St. Louis. That guy I told you about. The one with the tattoo? Been following us, he said."

"Was that the sounds we heard? Was it gunshots?"

Heddy nodded. She hit the town limit and picked up speed. Her hands were still shaking. She depended on Crow to do the killing. Until now she had never taken a life, though she'd thought of it often enough when she was thirteen and her mouth went dead.

"You just killed someone?" Jay asked.

"Jesus God," Carrie said and put her arm around Emily.

"I don't know if he was alone." Heddy put on the blinker and passed a car. She hadn't seen anyone following, but then she hadn't noticed anyone before either, yet he'd been there, tailing them for days.

"Shit." Crow leaned forward and touched her shoulder. "You okay?"

"A little shook. Not bad. I'll be okay."

"Someone must have heard those gunshots back at the station. They'll remember this car was there. They'll probably remember *you*." Jay turned toward Heddy in his seat, scrutinizing her as she drove.

"You turn the fuck around and watch the road! I won't

71

have you watching me," Heddy shouted. She pointed through the windshield and waited until he faced front again.

"This means they're really onto us, Heddy." Crow sounded nervous.

"Yeah, so the whole goddamn world's onto us, I don't care. We're getting out of here, we're going to Mexico, and any fucker tries to stop us is getting the same thing Rory got. No one's going to hurt us. No one's going to stop us."

She began to slow down and took the emergency lane, finally bringing the car to a stop. She took her hands from the wheel and rubbed down her face. Then she pulled open her damaged purse and found the bottle. She opened it and drank down what was left, gulping with her eyes closed.

"You want me to drive?" Crow asked.

"No. I'll drive. Give me a minute." She watched the mirrors and studied every car that passed by, wondering if any of the passengers might be from St. Louis. It occurred to her that the enemies she and Crow had made stealing the drug money were more of a problem than any law enforcement group. If they could walk right up to her at a bathroom in a service station . . .

"Heddy?"

"I'm going, I'm going." She put the car into gear and pulled back onto the highway.

"I can drive, you know," Crow said.

"I'm okay, I said!"

And she was. Or she would be. Just as soon as she got the buzz on and everything stopped being so sharp-edged and confusing.

Hell, why did everything have to be so goddamn complicated? Why didn't anything in her life ever go right?

She felt not so good. She felt pretty bad, really.

She felt like she would vomit or have a heart attack. She needed another bottle.

* * * * *

Heddy's mother was named Jolene and people called her Jo. When Heddy drove up to the door of the trailer where it sat on a little deserted patch of land outside of the small Kansas town, Jo waddled to the door and flung it wide. She squinted at the nice car. She walked out toward it, finally leaning down to peer through the windows. She saw Heddy.

Heddy waved a little, shut off the engine, and took the keys as she stepped out. "Mama," she called.

"Girl! I heard about Craig on the news. I wondered if that was you got him out."

"Crow, Mama. Call him Crow, okay?"

Jo returned to the trailer door and pushed two small mongrel dogs out of the way with her feet. She noticed a brown mess on her right shoe, backed out of the door. She stepped over to the edge of the metal platform and scraped it off. "Goddamn dog shit right where I got to walk. I swear to God I ought to eat them dogs for supper." She turned then and waited in front of the door for Heddy to approach. She held open her arms.

Heddy came forward slowly. She saw how the skin flapped beneath her mother's baggy arms. She was old, drunk, always drunk, and about as useless as any mother

73

could be. Heddy still cared, though she couldn't say why. It was perverse.

"Can we come in, Mama? We can't stay long."

" 'Cause you're on the run, huh, girl?"

Heddy nodded. "I guess so."

"I told you Cr . . . uh . . . Crow would get you in trouble one day."

Crow herded the family forward. He bowed to the old woman and said, "I love you too, Mama."

"Shut up, you wimpy asshole. C'mon on in, Heddy. I'll pour us a drink. Mind the dogs. One of 'em bites."

Heddy watched her mother open the door, scoop the two dogs into her arms, and then disappear into the gloom of the trailer. She turned to Crow, shrugged, and went inside too.

The rest followed, crowding into the tiny living room area littered with torn newspaper, dirty glasses, and dog excrement. Heddy stepped over a little pile that had dried to brown crust and dropped onto a gold and brown plaid sofa that she knew would make her skin itch. She watched Crow push Jay, Carrie, and the kid her way. They took seats, with the girl sitting in her mother's lap. Crow just stood near the door, scowling like an owl.

Jo was in the nearby kitchenette pouring two glasses of bourbon. "You want some, Crow? What about your friends, they need to wet the whistle?"

"Nah, not for me." Crow backed to the wall by the small television set and scooted down until he rested on his heels. "Not for them, either."

One of the dogs, a black and white spotted mixed terrier, came up to Crow and sniffed at his crotch. Crow bopped it on the head with his knuckles. It yipped and backed away.

"Don't be hurting my animals," Jo said, handing the

bourbon to her daughter. "Tell him he can get the hell out of my house if he's going to abuse my animals."

"Tell me yourself, Mama. I can hear you."

"Don't call me Mama. I would have smothered you at birth."

Heddy interrupted, saying, "Mama, I don't know when I'll get to see you again."

Jo drained her glass and wiped her mouth with the back of her hand before she said, "I don't reckon you ever came to see me much anyway."

"I know, but this is different. I have to go pretty far away."

"Will it be Canada or Mexico?"

"Look at her," Crow said. "Ain't she the smart one."

Without hesitation Jo whipped her empty glass around and threw it at Crow, narrowly missing his head. The glass struck the wall where it was soft from termite infestation, bounded off, and rolled over to Heddy's foot. She leaned over and retrieved it, handed it back to her mother. She mouthed, "Stop it" silently to Crow.

"Well?" her mother asked. "Canada or Mexico?"

"Does it matter? I just have to go. And I won't be coming back."

Jo turned, her loose flowered housedress flapping around her ankles, and found the bottle. She poured herself another shot.

"Who's all those tongue-tied people you got with you there? They going too?"

"Never mind about them, Mama, that's on a need-to-know basis and you don't need to know." Crow laughed at his little witticism, but not for long. Jo put down her glass on the counter very deliberately and reached over to the stove for a kettle of water. Steam rose from the spout.

"I was heating water for washing dishes, seeing as how my hot water heater's busted. But now that Crow's here, I think I can use this hot water for scrubbing out a dirty mouth and that would be a much better use for it."

Crow came up from the floor instantly, shaking his head. "Tell her to take it easy, Heddy. I'm in no mood for her games."

"You started it, Bully Boy," Jo said, advancing with the kettle swinging in her hand.

"Heddy, you tell her. Tell her now!" Crow reached into his satchel, feeling for his gun.

"Mama, that's enough. I didn't come to fight."

Jo halted and looked at her daughter. Her eyes slid over the other people on the sofa and stopped on the little girl.

"You got a kid," she said.

Heddy looked to where her mother's gaze was fastened. She said, "Yeah, that's her parents there."

"You took a kid?" Jo's words were slurring slightly and it was obvious to everyone by the way she swayed unevenly on her feet while holding the kettle aloft that she was not far away from a stupor.

"Heddy, we better go." Crow edged toward the door. Both dogs came to him, sniffing his pants legs and whining. He carefully pushed them away, a grimace on his face.

"Why'd you take a kid, Heddy? Damnit, girl, didn't I teach you anything? You don't mess with old people, cripples, and kids. You don't kick dogs and you don't lie to a priest. Those are the cardinal rules. You don't break them. What're you doing with that kid?"

"Mama, I don't want to get into that. Why don't you pour me another drink?" Heddy held out her empty glass. Her mother didn't look at it. She was still focused on Emily.

76

"What's your name, girl?" Jo asked.

Heddy stood up abruptly. "A drink, Mama? Want to pour me one?"

"Emily," Emily replied.

"That's a pretty name, Emily." Jo immediately turned on her daughter and jerked the hot kettle almost above her head. "I ought to scald you a new one, Heddy! What are you doing with Emily around a bastard like Crow? Have you lost what little brains you were born with?"

"Mama, put down the water." Heddy's voice was deep and dark and menacing. She stood her ground. "Put it back on the stove. Right now."

"I'll put it on the stove. After I douse you good, I'll put it back on the stove." She began to upturn the kettle, but just as the boiling liquid started out the spout, Heddy grabbed her mother's wrist and held on tightly.

"Put it down. In the kitchen, Mama."

Jo's eyes glazed over and then seemed to come to life again. "I have to put this down, it's killing my wrist," she said, turning when Heddy let her go and placing the kettle on the stove burner. "I'm so weak lately. I can't hold onto anything. It's hell getting old."

"Let's go, Heddy," Crow said again, fidgeting by the door, his hand on the door handle.

When her mother turned to her again, Heddy walked into her arms. She hugged her while the old woman stood there, her own arms limp at her side.

"I might call," Heddy said, stepping back. "Some day."

"Do you no good. I don't have a phone. They shut me off. You wouldn't have a few bucks to spare, would you? I'm all out of dog food and my animals are getting tired of eggs and bourbon shakes. Gives them the runs."

"Christ," Crow muttered, looking around with distaste

at the newspaper-strewn floors.

"He's no good, you know." Jo pointed a caffeine-stained forefinger at Crow. "He'll bring you down over this. He used you to get out and now he'll dump you or get you killed. But you got no right to take that kid into it. That's plain against the rules. I thought you had learned better."

"We'll let the kid go in a little while, don't worry about her. Listen, Mama, take this money." Heddy reached into her purse and withdrew a wad of bills.

"Oh boy. Where'd you get this?"

"It doesn't matter, keep it. Buy yourself a phone. Get dog food. Whatever. And maybe I'll call one day." Heddy turned and motioned for the Anderson family to rise. She marched them out the door behind Crow, who was the first through the opening.

Jo reached down and hugged the dogs to her chest so they wouldn't follow. She stepped to the door with them in her arms. On the path outside, Heddy turned and said, "You're no good either, Mama. No better than Crow. And I loved you too, no matter what. At least I was good for something."

She left her mother standing with her mouth hanging open and the dogs whining in her arms. She slammed the car door and viciously turned the ignition key. She revved the motor good and loud.

She sat a moment, thinking very bad thoughts. She thought if anyone in the car said one word to her, she'd take out her gun and kill him for it. One word. Any word. Boo. Love. Mother. Drunk. Filthy. Ignorant. Pitiful. Slow. Backward. Trashy. Crazy. Any word at all. Let one of them say something. And she'd kill him. It wouldn't take two seconds.

* * * * *

Hawkins watched the little girl tell him about the murder Heddy committed at the gas station. Then the tale of the side trip to see Heddy's mother in Kansas. What a downward spiral this family's life had taken once in the clutches of an escaped convict and his lethal girlfriend. The more that was revealed, the more Frank wondered at Emily's resilience.

When Jay found out that Heddy killed the drug chemist sent to recover the stolen money at the service station, did he admire the woman in some way? Maybe he started to empathize with her as she took down the "bad guy" and protected herself and the loot. It was, after all, dirty money, up for grabs. Combined with her mysterious and strange sexual bravado, her willingness to use deadly force might have seemed alluring to a man teetering on the edge.

His own wife presented no challenge, and in fact her very acquiescence infuriated Jay. Heddy, on the other hand, moved around in the same dangerous world as Jay, albeit on the other side of the law.

Frank really wanted to get a handle on what happened in that car on the flight to Mexico so he could understand how a twelve-year law enforcement veteran ended up ready to throw away his family and his life in order to be a part of the criminal underground.

It was always possible, it occurred to Frank, that this wasn't the first time Jay had walked on the dark side. There was no evidence, but perhaps Jay had already been dealing with drug dealers or thieves, taking kickbacks or bargaining for a piece of the illegal profits. Even in a small town there was money under the table changing hands. People didn't talk about it, but everyone knew there was a whole underground network that infiltrated both sides of the law when it came to drugs.

Frank had casually asked Jay, "Do you like your job?"

It was usual the patient lied when asked this, because with Frank being tied to law enforcement he held the patient's future in his hands. He could recommend the officer be let go.

Despite that possibility, Jay answered as truthfully as Frank thought he could have under the circumstances.

"I used to."

"Does that mean you don't like it anymore?"

Jay wouldn't meet his gaze. "It's harder to like it."

"Talk to me about the problems you think you're having with your job."

Jay barked out a harsh laugh. "Money, for starters. I'm shopping for a new car, trying to trade in our old one. You have any idea what new cars cost? Not much less than my yearly salary. It's going to make us skimp on other things in order to get one. My old car is a piece of crap and worth hardly nothing."

"Your wife works, doesn't she?" Frank pushed aside papers in Jay's folder looking for the information he wanted. "She teaches school . . ."

"Yeah, and you want to know what teachers make?"

"Point taken. All right, there are money worries. Anything else about your work you want to talk about?"

"I'm getting tired of being despised."

"How do you mean?"

80

"When I first came on the force people showed some respect for cops. You know how they are now. To the public we're about one notch above the killers and rapists. They don't trust us, they don't want to see us unless they call and then they want us there in two minutes flat to lay our lives on the line for their safety."

"You resent your place in society."

"I guess you could say that. Were you ever on the street?"

Frank sat back from the force of Jay's vehemence. There was enough anger there to blow fuses. "I was on the street early on, sure. It was some time back . . ."

"Then you don't know what I'm saying. If you haven't been out there lately and felt that disdain, you can't imagine how thick it is."

"I'd think in a small town such as yours . . ."

"It's no different! I've had grade school kids call me pig, the homeless, what few we have, spit on me, and one rich society bitch threatened she'd get my badge if I didn't agree *cheerfully* to keep a round-the-clock watch on her palatial home while she flew off to Paris for two weeks."

"That's tough," Frank remarked, having heard some of these same complaints before. He knew it was no picnic out there, big city or small town, but Jay's anger was out of all proportion to the perceived insults he suffered from "the public." He was walking around with a chip on his shoulder so big it was about to topple him over.

When Frank carefully suggested that maybe Jay should think of looking for another line of work, he grew abusive.

"Yeah, why don't I go for your job? Sit in a nice office with bookcases and an intercom. Spend my days safe and warm, listening to sob stories."

"Is that called for?" Frank asked.

Jay stood and paced around the small office. "Maybe not. You asked how I feel and what about thinking of another job. I'm sorry, I seem to blow like this all the time. It's why I'm here, isn't it? As for other work, I'm not trained for anything else. I guess I could go into security, but I *hate* that. It's about as exciting as branding cows on a farm. And pays about the same, too."

Frank concluded that Jay could turn into a dangerous man. Feeling trapped and unappreciated, in need of more money for a better lifestyle, furious with his stake in life, he was ripe for some kind of fall.

Frank's attention came back to the little girl's story. After cold-blooded murder, and the stop at Heddy's mother's trailer, what had Heddy and Crow done then? And what was Jay's part in it?

It was important to know as much as he could find out. He'd had a stake in Jay Anderson for months and the books couldn't be closed until he found a way to understand how it all came down.

* * * * *

Throughout the long day Heddy drove relentlessly, her silence a heavy cloud that hovered over and informed the other occupants of the car. She stopped for gas once where she and Crow took their hostages to the bathroom one by one. She stopped again for food around noon, hotdogs and fries and shakes at the drive up window of a Sonic.

By afternoon even Crow had grown morose from

spending hours trapped in the silent car. He began to complain, at first in a joking way and, then, when Heddy did not respond, more noisily.

"I can't take another hour in this car, Heddy. You're going to have to give it a break."

Heddy failed to reply. She drove steadily, her hands gripped hard on the steering wheel. She smelled of booze and desperation. The combination cast a sour scent over the air inside the car.

"Heddy, now goddamnit, you let that dead son of a bitch back there throw you like this and it's not going to help our chances. Or if it's that thing with your Mom, hell, brush it off. She can't help herself. But whatever it is, I have to tell you I *am not* going to sit in this car every day while you fucking sulk."

"She's thinking how much she likes me," Jay said.

"Oh your mouth," Crow said, fairly shouting. "He's getting to you, Heddy. I can't believe you're letting him do that."

"I'm finding a place to stay the night," Heddy said quietly. "If you'll *just shut up*. Christ, I get tired of trying to get y'all to shut up."

Crow jerked back in the seat and sat fuming. He had tied a dozen knots in the leather straps of his shoulder bag. Now he set about untying them to keep from hitting someone in the face. He knew he was dangerously close to losing it and he didn't want to do that. He never should have done more crank when he knew there was this much tension. Speed put him out of control—what he usually wanted—but he'd made a mistake doing so much of the drug while trapped in a car, unable to move around and let out the streams of energy that rolled off him like clouds of steam.

Within fifteen minutes of announcing she was going to

stop, Heddy slowed in a small town just over the border in Oklahoma. She found a little motel on the outskirts and got a room with two double beds. Once they were all inside, she stood with her hands on her hips to address Crow.

"We're being followed."

Surprise corralled his face, pulled it down and threw it in the way you hog-tie a calf and throw it to the ground under the five-second bell. "You know that for sure?"

Heddy saw Jay grinning and pointed to him. "He knows it. It's a little dark blue car. It picked us up not far outside that town where I had to shoot Rory. It must have followed us to my Mom's and waited somewhere."

"So they know you stopped here, at this motel. Jesus Christ, Heddy . . . !"

"Whoever it is, they would have known no matter where we stopped. What we have to do now is stay on watch."

"I dunno . . . maybe if we offered to give the money ba . . ."

"Crow!"

His head came up at how she'd interrupted him. "What?"

"We ain't giving back nothing, nothing, you hear me? It's ours. We need it and we're keeping it. So just get that out of your head."

"You took something you shouldn't have," Jay said in a voice that showed he was interested in all the details. "It's not the cops you're worried about now, is it? Don't you know you're involving innocent people in your screwed up little affairs? You need to let my wife and child go at least."

"Tie him up," Heddy commanded. "I'm going out to find something to eat."

Crow bound Jay and pushed him onto one of the beds. He left Carrie and Emily free. He started pacing the room, passing the bed where Jay lay, and watching him carefully

84

the way a hyena watches a wounded antelope on a wide-open plain.

"What'd she get you into?" Jay asked. "I know you do what she says and you think she's bright, but now she's dropped you into a world of trouble, hasn't she? How smart is that? Maybe you ought to try making your own decisions for a change."

Crow passed a small lamp on a table opposite the bed, grabbed it, ripped the cord from the wall, and hurled the lamp at Jay's head. It missed, muddy brown glass shattering against the headboard. Carrie gasped and Emily let out a short scream before she covered her mouth with her hand.

"Go ahead," Crow warned. "Keep it up and see what it gets you. Talk about Heddy some more, why don't you? Bad mouth her when her back's turned. You think I don't know what you're doing? Split us, turn us against one another, that's what you're doing. I'm not completely STUPID! Do I have a sign on my back saying I just joined the human race?"

Jay kept quiet. He glanced at his wife and back at Crow still standing over the end of the bed, furiously slapping at one thigh with his hand, the repetitive action a nervous tic.

"I'm not saying a thing," Jay finally said.

"It's about goddamn time, man. I get tired of it and there's no predicting what I might want to do to you. But it won't be pretty so keep it zipped, okay?"

"Must be the mob you stole something from," Jay said.

"Oh *man!*" Crow was on the bed like a flash, pummeling Jay in the gut with both fists while calling him names and threatening to shut his mouth permanently. Jay's hands were tied behind his back and all he could do was head-butt and knee the other man. Carrie rushed to rescue her husband and Emily was at her mother's back, trying to pull her away from the melee.

Carrie hauled back on Crow's leather vest until he slipped to the floor. He jumped to his feet, fists up, glaring at her. "I ought to give you some of it," he said.

"Please, please," she said, "can't you stop this, can't you just stop it? Please, stop it." Tears slipped down her face, making snail tracks of silver over the tanned smooth planes of her cheeks.

It was as if window shades had snapped up in the depths of Crow's eyes to let in the light of reason. His fists relaxed and he stepped around the bed. Carrie tried to turn away to wipe her face. He put his arms around her body, pulling her into his embrace. She turned her head away from him and he reached up and brought her face back to his own. He looked down into wet brown eyes and said, "You're a good woman, taking up for your man that way. I've always been a fool for good women."

Carrie tried to break away, but he held her. Then he leaned forward and pressed his lips on hers. When he was done, he let her go so that she stumbled back. Crow turned to Jay on the bed where he was trying to get back his breath from the beating he'd taken. "You see what I did? You need lessons or something? You hit a woman like this, you bastard? Even I wouldn't hit this woman. And you think you're better than I am, don't you? You're the law, you're The Man, and I'm this scum you like to step on. But I'd never hit a woman willing to stand up for me. Where does that put you on the scale, man? Live with that, why don't you?"

Crow spit toward the bed then moved to the window to look out for Heddy. A war between hatred and passion fought on in his brain so that he couldn't look at Jay or he might kill him, and he couldn't look at the woman or he might want to take her. Here, now, no matter what anybody thought.

* * * * *

It was like Crow was a wild puppet. Someone invisible pulled his strings and he danced. When he went for Daddy in the motel room that second night, I thought he was going to kill him then. How many times now had I worried my parents would be killed and they'd survived? It was like watching Wily Coyote falling off cliffs, blowing himself up, getting flattened by anvils. He died and he died and he died trying to catch the Roadrunner, but he didn't really die.

I was afraid I'd start thinking that way about us. If we kept getting close and yet not dying, maybe it wasn't real. But it was, the threat was very real and every time Crow attacked Daddy I thought it was for the last time. It made my whole insides go crazy. I got gas and had to go to the bathroom to pass it so no one would hear. I think it's real nasty and embarrassing to pass gas in company. I'd just want to die if I did it in front of anyone. I got a headache and stomachaches and even my legs started hurting, I don't know why.

It's real hard on you to want to get away from someone and you can't. Your whole body gets tight so that your fingers twitch and your neck shrinks down into your shoulders and your stomach's always doing flip-flops or knotting up. I could put my hand flat on my stomach and feel the knot, like it was a ball of string I'd swallowed in my sleep.

When we'd stopped at the trailer where Heddy's mother lived with the dogs and the messy stuff on the floor, I think we all lost our tongues. Mama and Daddy never said a word. Not even when we left and we could see how upset Heddy was. I told the woman my name and she got onto Heddy for keeping me hostage, but it didn't do any good. I could tell it wouldn't. I had gotten some of the cold thoughts streaming off Heddy when we were on our way again and I could tell she'd never listened to her mother, about anything. She thought her mother didn't love her. She thought she was unlovable and ugly and she was so full of hatred that I knew none of us better say anything to her. It took hours for her to snap out of it and find a motel.

When Heddy came back to the motel she brought Popeye's Fried Chicken, red beans and rice, and coleslaw. No one could eat a thing except Crow. He ate like a big dog, shoving it in, eating with his mouth open, making smacking, chewing noises. I had to look away from him to even get myself to take a bite from a chicken leg. I guess nobody ever taught him any table manners. Maybe he never had a mother or father to teach him. Maybe he was one of those runaway kids who grow up on the streets—like Daddy called him—a gutter punk. Still, didn't he know how awful it was to watch him eat with his mouth open?

After we ate, Crow tied us up and then Heddy brought out a big razor machine from a shopping bag. It was a scary looking thing, black, with a row of teeth along the edge. If she had wanted to torture us, that was the instrument to use, it seemed to me.

Crow grabbed his hair in both hands and said, "No, uh-uh."

"You keep that hair and you'll wear it back to prison. Or worse."

"What could be worse?"

"The lab people catch us."

Daddy lifted his head from the bed. "Lab?"

"Ignore him," Heddy said, frowning at Daddy.

"I might take off a couple inches," Crow said, eyeing the electric razor.

"You'll take it all off. I'll give you a buzz cut. Let's go in the bathroom so you can sit on the toilet seat."

Crow grumbled and swore, but he let his hair be cut off until all he had left was a half-inch of fuzzy black like a monk's cap covering his head. When he looked in the mirror, he yelled and stomped into the room where we were lying on the beds. He was shocking looking, all bare headed like that.

"This is for shit, I look like a skin head, I look like a Jew ready for the showers! I never should have let you talk me into it."

I almost laughed seeing him. He looked like a kid who just joined the Army. His ears were too big, sticking out from his head like Dumbo, the elephant. His eyebrows were real thick, black as worms covered in dirt. Everything about his face looked too large and cartoonish without the long wavy hair that had made him look almost handsome in a hoody-street-boy sort of way.

"Take off the earrings too," Heddy said. "And go through Jay's suitcase, find one of his shirts to wear. Hang up that vest, we'll leave it here. It smells anyway."

"Why do I have to do everything? What about you?" He reached up to slip out the silver arrows dangling on chains from his pierced earlobes.

"The cops don't have photographs of me."

"But the guys in St. Louis know you."

Heddy rustled in the shopping bag lying on the table and brought out a wig. It was short, dark brown, and curly, like the head of a mop. Her own hair was long and sandy blond; it fell in a part in the middle of her head and looked like it needed a good cut. "I didn't forget," she said. She waved the wig at him.

"Maybe you could have bought me a wig too, goddamn it."

Heddy moved up to him and circled her arms around his waist. "Now, now. Who's your baby?"

The wig hung from her hands behind his back now. She kissed Crow, opening her mouth so I saw her long pink tongue. They kissed for a long time. I watched. I couldn't stop watching them. They weren't like anyone I'd ever known. Being with them was like visiting a weird people zoo and getting a chance to look at the new freaks on exhibit someone had found in some strange country I didn't even know the name of.

When she stepped away from him, she put on the wig, struggling to tuck her own hair beneath it. She looked like Shirley Temple from those old black-and-white movies my Mama watched on TV sometimes. *Little Miss Marker*. Except for her mouth—that made her ugly and not at all like a little girl in a picture show.

Crow laughed at seeing her. They began a pinching contest. First he reached over and pinched her boob and then she pinched the skin on his belly, then he pinched her earlobe. They chased one another around the room, hopping on the beds, stepping over us, pinching and playing chase and laughing out loud to beat the band, just like kids do.

I have to tell you something now I don't know you'll understand. While Crow and Heddy were playing games and acting funny, I started liking them. I don't mean that I liked them a lot or anything, or wasn't scared of them anymore. But just for those few minutes I realized they used to be little kids who had never done anything wrong, kids with their whole lives before them. Those kids were inside them now, prisoners, just like my Daddy's nice little kid-self was inside him, hidden away. And my Mama's brave little kid-self was inside her, staying quiet so no one knows it's there, no one knows how much courage she has.

Do grown-ups all have their kid-selves inside them yet? I didn't know, but that's what it looked like. Crow-the-kid and Heddy-the-kid got loose that evening in the motel room and there they were, wearing wigs and thinking up disguises and playing chase like nothing in the world was wrong with them that couldn't be fixed.

Then Crow did something that made me stop liking the silly kid games they were playing. He hopped on the bed where Mama was sitting and pinned her on her back. He called to Heddy, "You think it's time I sample this one?"

"Hey, go for it. Fair's fair."

Before I knew it, I was out of the chair and pulling on his arm, trying to get him off my Mama. Daddy was up too, off the side of the other bed and reaching across the mattress saying, "You don't touch her, you bastard."

Crow pushed Daddy away, causing him to fall back. Heddy said in a deep voice, "You move away." We turned to see her and she had a small handgun pointed at Daddy. "Fair's fair, I said. Get over there, on the other bed, *now*."

Crow crawled off Mama and stood between the beds, tying Daddy's hands behind him and his feet at the ankles. Daddy said, "You better not do it."

"Hide and watch, Jaybird."

With Daddy all tied up, Heddy got hold of the back of

my hair and marched me toward the bathroom. I said, crying now cause I couldn't help it, "Don't hurt my Mama."

"No one's hurting nobody. Get the hell in there." She pushed me inside and shut the door. She called through it, "And don't come out unless I tell you to."

"Leave my Mama alone!"

Crow must have changed his mind. Or came to his senses. Or something. Because I stood a long time with the side of my face pressed against the door, listening, and I heard them talking—Crow and my Mama. I couldn't stop crying. Snot was running down over my lip and I blubbered like a stupid little kid. Hadn't I known Crow would do it? Hadn't I warned Mama?

I'm so glad Crow didn't do what he was thinking of doing. I heard him say, finally, "Oh hell, I was only kidding. I'm not going to do nothing. Shit. It was a joke."

You have to know my Mama to know how really bad a thing it was Crow had threatened to do. She told me once how she'd never had real boyfriends until she met my father. How she loved him more than life itself in the beginning. I think even though she was going to leave him after our vacation trip, she still loved him and no one else. She sure didn't love Crow; she was scared of him. Forced to have sex with him, nobody to help her, no way to stop him, while Heddy looked on . . . Well, it was the worst thing that might have happened. I don't know how she did it, but Mama talked him out of it.

"We can stop for a while if you want to." The psychologist handed me his handkerchief. He smoked and paced and moved his hands around like he didn't know where to put them.

No, it's all right, I want to tell you the rest of what happened that night, I said, mopping my face dry and sitting up straight in the chair. Just thinking about that night made me cry. Mama was the most innocent one of us all. Even I understood bad people and how the world is a crazy place better than Mama did. The threat of something bad happening to her was just too much, even when talking about it.

Anyway, I said, they didn't keep me in the bathroom long. The games all stopped when there was a knock on the door.

Crow was suddenly at the bathroom door, opening it and putting his finger to his lips to make sure I didn't say anything. His face was serious again, and it was the color of ashes in a fireplace. He reached into his satchel he carried in his arms and brought out a gun. It was my Daddy's gun, the Smith and Wesson.

"It's your friends," Daddy said. I could see him lying tied up on the bed. I looked at the other bed for Mama. She had curled into a ball, her back to me, the cover pulled up to her neck. She was all right, but she didn't want to talk to Crow anymore. Or anyone else.

I wanted to run to her, but Crow pushed me up against the sink and blocked my way. I really hated him. If I had been big as he was, I would have hurt him any way I could. I never felt that way before, where I wanted to hurt someone. It made me mad Crow caused me to have those feelings. I'd promised myself I'd never be like Daddy, hurting people when I felt like it.

Daddy said again, when the knock came, "Must be your friends." I don't know why he kept pushing them. He couldn't help it, I guess, especially now they'd threatened and scared Mama. Every chance he got he said stuff to them that made them mad enough to kill him. This time, though, neither of them paid him any mind. They were just too busy figuring out what to do. I could see neither of them had a clue what the knocking on the door meant.

Crow slipped from the bathroom to the motel door and stood beside it, the gun raised. He nodded his head at Heddy to stay back and say something. She called out, "Who is it?"

"Manager. I forgot to write down your driver's license number, ma'am."

Heddy took a deep breath and Crow moved back from the door. He returned to the bathroom with me and closed the door part way, the light off so he could watch. Heddy got her wallet from her purse and went to unlock the door. I remember thinking she must have all kinds of false ID. She couldn't very well show them a license under her real name.

I didn't like being in a dark room with Crow. His pants were sagging over his skinny behind because he hadn't taken time to put on his belt. He was fidgeting, the gun moving in rapid little jerks in his hand. I moved to where I could see out, trying not to watch how Crow was behaving.

As soon as Heddy had the safety chain off and the door open a crack, she was pushed back, the door forced in toward her. A man with a black gun with a long barrel on it came into the room and shut the door behind him. He had on tight jeans and a brown tee shirt. He looked like a college kid, kind of cute. He had blue eyes with long black lashes and he smiled pretty, even if the smile didn't go with the scary-looking gun in his hand.

Heddy said, "What the hell you think you're doing?"

The man took in Daddy tied on one bed and Mama covered up on the other, then he looked at the bathroom door and must have seen Crow. He reached out to grab Heddy.

That's when there was a shot that made my ears ring and . . . and . . .

. . . I don't have to tell you how it looked, do I? You've seen that stuff before, haven't you? As a policeman? When people get shot? I never thought I'd ever see real blood, see real people shot and dying.

What happened next went real fast. I could hardly keep up, trying to see what was going on. My heart was beating like crazy and I realized I was holding my breath.

The man was down and Heddy kicked away his gun. Crow came out of the bathroom, shaking his head, mumbling curses.

"Get him untied," Heddy said, motioning at Daddy. "We've got to get outta here."

Daddy was pushing them again by saying stuff, but they acted like they didn't even hear him. We were out of the motel room and on the road within minutes, I don't even know how we moved that fast. I had to help Mama. She wasn't . . . she wasn't all the way buttoned up . . . She kept saying, "Hush, baby, hush," even though I wasn't saying anything.

I couldn't stop remembering the college boy on the floor where we stepped over him. He really looked like someone who should have had books in his hand, not a gun. I thought all criminals were slimy looking. On TV and in the movies the bad guys wear dirty clothes and they look all crooked and beat up. They frown, not smile; they have scars and pimples and pockmarks. I was figuring out that bad people looked like the rest of us most of the time. That wasn't fair. You'd never be able to tell one from the other. You'd never know when to be afraid.

The boy we left in the motel room had a hole in his belly and his hands over it. He was moaning, but not very loud.

Blood came from between his fingers and dripped around them back onto his dark shirt. I couldn't see his eyes, his face was turned to the wall and his knees were drawn up.

I thought Heddy and Crow would help him, but they wanted us out of there. Away from there. Someone would have come to investigate the sound of the gunshot. Heddy and Crow didn't have time to check on the man who had probably been about to shoot them anyway. That's what they said when I asked them. That's what they told me.

"You don't stop to call an ambulance for a guy who would have shot you dead," Crow said. "Let's get our priorities straight, kid."

Heddy drove too fast. The car felt like it was a rocket ship roaring down the road. She passed every car in sight while Crow talked and talked and talked. He was a tape machine, turned on to fast forward. Daddy talked some more too, but no one listened to him, like he was a turned off machine or he was speaking behind a screen or something.

I thought we were going to have a wreck, Heddy drove so fast.

And then we did.

One moment she had it under control. The next moment she had hit a deep puddle of water standing on the highway from a shower earlier in the evening, and the car was hydroplaning across the center dividing line toward an oncoming car.

Heddy screamed, over-compensated on the wheel, hit the brakes, and the Riviera fishtailed despite the new, supposedly safer brake system. The oncoming vehicle, an old Volkswagen bus, nicked the rear panel of the Riviera and both of the cars caromed off the pavement and back onto it again. Two other cars, each coming from opposite directions, slammed on brakes, but entered the maelstrom nonetheless.

For several moments the occupants of the Riviera rode a rollercoaster ride, taking jolts that threw them against the car doors, the dash, the wheel, and even the roof of the car. Heddy had both feet on the brake, had it stomped clear down to the floor, her teeth clamped shut and grinding, her mind going blank, all time telescoping into a few infinitesimal moments.

Rending metal screamed like train wheels braking on hot rails and cracking safety glass spidered, then popped. The twin air bags in the front seat exploded with a loud whooshing sound of air, covering and pressing both Heddy and Jay back into their bucket seats, burning their faces, scaring the life out of them.

Seconds later one of the two air bags in the back seat exploded into Crow's face, knocking him sideways into the door. His head banged against the window so hard he was knocked out instantly. Emily was thrown to the floorboard and Carrie was flung across the seat lengthwise, her head landing against the inflated air bag.

Finally, after what seemed an interminable length of time, all the motion stopped and the car died.

It was a five-car pile-up. From Heddy's vantage point it seemed to her the driver of the Volkswagen was dead. A matron with steel silver hair slumped over the steering wheel with her skull cracked on the windshield. Blood ran from the wound to cover her face.

People in the remaining three cars were in various con-ditions from dead (a teen male driver of an older model Mitsubishi Galant), to slightly injured (his passenger, a young girl who looked to have suffered mere bruises where the seatbelt held her in position during the crash.) In the third car, a white Chevrolet Caprice, the driver and passenger, two men, seemed shaken but unharmed. The front of their car had bumper damage and the hood was crimped, but otherwise they had come into the wreck at a slower rate of speed and had been able to avoid the worst of it.

Cars stopped, halted by the debris and carnage blocking the highway, drivers stepping out of their vehicles to lend a hand.

Heddy pushed and finally got the air bag out of her face and to the side. She put both hands against her cheeks. They felt hot to the touch and raw, as if the first layer of her skin had been peeled off. Tears blinded her until she rubbed them from her eyes.

She looked around the interior of the Riviera. Panic overrode the first adrenaline rush of fear that had taken her when she hit the water and went into the slow-motion spin. *Have to get out of the car. Cops will come soon.* Over and over, that's all she could think, *get out, get away, hurry.*

She saw Jay pawing his way from beneath the air bag and said to him, "Get out of the car and to the side of the road. Wait there. You say a fucking word to anyone, I'll shoot Emily in the head and I mean it."

He twisted in his seat to see his family. His face was also burned red from the impact of the exploding air bag, but he seemed not to notice it. "Em? Carrie?"

"I'm all right, Daddy." Emily peeked up from behind the

seat. "I just bumped my head and my knees, I think." Her voice was shaky.

"I hurt my arm," Carrie said, rising from where she lay across the seat, holding onto her left arm.

"Get out of the car!" Heddy roared.

Jay fumbled for the door and unlocked it, then stumbled out.

Heddy couldn't get her door open. She realized after a struggle that it must be crushed in. She caught a glimpse of other people in the several car lights that lit up the highway and the wrecks. It looked like a nightmare to her. She wished she was dreaming, but she knew this was for real and they were in pretty deep trouble. Someone might be dead (the driver of the Volkswagen and the kid in the Galant) and maybe someone in the cars stopping on each side of the wrecked cars had a cellular phone and was already calling the cops.

She crawled across the center console between the front bucket seats and out Jay's side. She hurried around the car to where Crow was. He sat with his head against the spider-cracked window, perfectly still, his eyes closed. The air bag was crumpled all around him, like a cushion an assassin had pressed down around his head. She jerked open the door and had to catch him as he fell toward her. "Crow! Wake up, get up, Crow, are you all right? Damnit, damnit!"

His eyes slowly opened and then he blinked several times as if he didn't know her. Finally he said, "We still alive?" His upper teeth must have bitten down on his lower lip because it bled a bright red stream down his chin and neck.

"Come on, try to stand up. They'll be cops here soon. We have to get away from here."

He pulled himself up by holding onto the door. He surveyed the damage to the car and, with Heddy, realized that it was totaled. The front end was crushed, the driver's door was bent in the middle, and along the side of the car were streaks of metal scraped bare. All the windows were either broken or half missing. "Christ, Heddy . . ."

"Let's go." She reached into the back seat and withdrew his leather satchel. "Here, take this, move it!"

Heddy knew she possessed the coolest head and she had no injuries beyond the facial burns, at least she couldn't feel anything else wrong yet. It was up to her to get them out of this.

She hurried Crow away from the car, avoiding the head-lights, and over to the side of the road. Someone came up to them, an elderly man in overalls. He said, "You're hurt, let me help you."

Heddy snarled, "Get the fuck away from me, man," and he backed away, surprised.

Crow was stumbling, but his steps were surer as they reached the gravel lining the road where Jay stood holding Emily in his arms. Next to him stood Carrie shivering, keeping her arm close to her body. Jay was already sur-veying the wrecked cars, looking for someone to help them, someone to report to, Heddy saw it in his face.

"Move it," she said, slipping her free hand into her purse. It was a new one she'd bought at a discount depart-ment store when she had gone out earlier to pick up the chicken for dinner. It was a big forest green vinyl bag and it held, besides the money and her gun, two pints of Jim Beam from a local liquor store. It seemed a lifetime ago that every-thing had started going wrong. The guy at the service sta-tion surprising her at the ladies' room door. The boy who stepped into the room with a gun to which a silencer had been attached. And now this . . .

She herded the family before her and steadied Crow with

one hand on his upper arm. They passed by the other wrecked cars, scurrying along. Heddy saw the female driver of the Volkswagen and knew she was either dead or completely knocked senseless. She wasn't moving while two men tried to pry open her stuck driver's door. She saw the kid in the Galant, his girlfriend on her knees in the front seat, hanging over him and wailing. People were at her door, trying to convince her to come out of the car. Spilled gasoline from ruptured tanks created rainbow sheets sparkling across the pavement. Heddy wrinkled her nose at the stink. The whole place could go up with one spark. *Outta here, have to get away from here.*

All total there were probably eight cars and trucks at the scene, but most everyone had exited their vehicles to try to help the people still remaining in the wrecked cars. They paid scant attention to the five stragglers making their way past the stalled cars into the darkness beyond. Too many people all over the place, too much activity.

Heddy looked around and saw the road was bounded on one side by a forest and on the other by open fields. She said, "We'll head across the road, into those trees."

They lost the glow of headlights as they moved deeper into tree cover. The land was flat and it was clear between trees, so the going was easy. After they were in a couple of hundred yards, Heddy told Jay to turn right. She hoped they were following the road and could come out far enough away from the wreck to catch a ride. Not catch a ride, actually, but take one.

Her face kept burning so that she put her hand up to her cheeks over and over, wondering how bad it looked, how red it was. Yet they'd been lucky, all of them, to escape serious injury.

They could get away from this mess if they hurried.

101

They were behind the highway patrol's back if she was right about this maneuver. Who the hell knew? She was like some kind of glider that sailed in the clouds, going whatever way the wind blew.

Carrie was making sounds. Heddy said, "Shut up, you're not hurt."

"Where are we going?" Jay asked, but he continued walking.

Crow kept wiping his lip and saying, "Shit, I'm all bloody, shit, look at this shit, how'd that happen, Heddy?"

"It was an accident, how'd you think it happened? No, really, I decided there wasn't enough excitement and thought I'd plow into an oncoming car. You dumb fucking goof."

"Can the comedy, will you? Where we going?" Crow wanted to know, unconsciously echoing Jay.

"I hope we're following alongside the road and we can come out above the wreck. I'll flag down a car."

"Maybe you'll flag down a patrol car," Jay said. "Maybe you better flag down an ambulance. My wife's hurt and Emily might be hurt too."

"I'm okay, Daddy."

Just then they heard the sirens and knew the ambulances and cops were closing in. Everyone stopped, even Heddy, to listen. She judged they were too far away to ever find them now. She couldn't even make out any individual lights from the direction of the highway, only a hazy yellow glow that came through the tops of the trees. At any moment she expected to hear an explosion and the whole area light up with flame.

She pushed them onward and for another twenty minutes they walked through dark, silent woods, no sounds other than their feet on the soft cushiony leaf fall on the ground and an occasional whimper from Carrie. Even the kid was quiet, walking next to her father, holding onto his hand to keep from falling in the dark.

When Heddy thought they were far enough from the scene, she instructed Jay to head back toward the highway. At the woods' edge, she turned to Crow and put both hands on his shoulders to look into his face. "You okay now? Can you keep an eye on them until I get another car?"

He grinned a little then winced and wiped at his split lip. "Yeah, I got it wrapped."

"I wish that was true." With that she stepped away from the treeline and crossed a soggy drainage ditch, her shoes sinking and squishing, to the roadside. She saw a car coming toward her, its headlights small white eyes cutting through the darkness. There was no lighted bubble on top so she hoped it wasn't a patrol car. If it was . . . hell, she'd know what to do if it came to that. You did what you had to. That's what she and Crow had been doing for days now. Whatever the situation called for, they did it. You didn't survive any other way.

She stepped onto the macadam and felt the heat of it warm the soles of her muddy shoes. Despite the earlier rain, the highway retained sunny summer heat even as the night lengthened. She was sweating a ton of fear sweat, though the air had cooled. She could smell herself, an acrid musky scent crawling all over her body. She didn't know how she looked. She had on the wig and had straightened it before leaving the woods. But she might have blood on her from Crow and her face was probably scarlet with burns. She had no idea. She just knew she had a mission to perform, and she'd do that. Nothing could stop her. Not now, not ever.

As the car neared, slowing, she stepped further into the road, blocking passage, and waved her arms. The car lights were in her eyes, white sapphire suns bearing down out of darkness. The car stopped. She rushed toward it and around to the driver's side. She had the gun out before she got there and hit the rolled up window with the gun barrel. The driver was a woman, fortyish, her eyes big and round with new fear.

"Open the goddamn door." Could she shoot this woman? She didn't think so. Or maybe she could. Yes, she could. If she had to, she'd shoot her.

The woman started moving the car forward and Heddy stepped back, taking aim, ready to put a bullet through the window. The woman watched her and slammed the brakes. The car, a very old red Ford Escort, died.

"Get out of the car," Heddy shouted. She looked up and down the rural two-lane highway, hoping no one else would come along. "Hurry!"

The woman unlocked her door and stepped out. Heddy marched her at gunpoint across the ditch to where Crow waited with the others. "Go get in the car, I'll take care of this." Crow took the woman driver by an arm.

The woman was babbling. She had been terrified when the red-faced stranger pointed a weapon at her, but now that she saw so many people, some of them dripping blood or looking wounded, Heddy could see she was wild with panic. Her hands fluttered at her breast as if they would be able to catch reality and bend it back to normal again.

Heddy gestured the family to the car. She got them inside and tried the ignition. It started on the first try, but it backfired and boiled smoke from the exhaust. She put it into gear and heard the clunk, felt the lurch jerk her backward as the transmission dropped into drive. She had to get it turned around and pointed back the way it had come, away from the accident scene ahead.

"What a piece of shit. I had to stop a car that ought to be in a junkyard, for crying out loud!" She turned the car in a circle and kept it idling by placing one foot on the brake while pressing on the gas pedal to keep the engine going, waiting for Crow. She thought at first the sound she heard was another backfire, but then she realized the sound had come from the forest where she couldn't see a thing.

Crow killed the woman. Well, she wasn't surprised. The woman would have told the cops her car had been stolen; she would have let everyone know what car they were in. Shit happens, that was Heddy's philosophy. It happens to the best of us, she thought. Don't it, though? Life's a beach and then you drown. What a hoot.

If she wasn't so exhausted, so wired and sick to her stomach and trembling with an overload of adrenaline, she'd laugh at just how many people were dying tonight. It was a regular slaughter.

* * * * *

The Escort wouldn't go over fifty miles an hour. At that speed it rumbled and spit coal black smoke from the exhaust pipes and threatened to shake itself to pieces.

"You couldn't find a better car than this?" Crow asked. He wished now he'd let Heddy stay in the woods and he'd been the one to approach the road to flag down a vehicle.

"It's not my fault that woman was driving this junk heap. How is it my fault? Shit."

There had been headlights behind them for twenty miles

now. Another junk heap unable to go very fast, Crow wondered? Or their pals from St. Louis who always seemed to be on their tail?

"Well, we're gonna have to do something, Heddy. I think we've got company on our ass."

He saw Heddy glance in the rearview mirror. The car jerked and banged as she tried to push it above fifty. Suddenly she applied the brakes and they all found their heads whip-lashing. She pulled to the side of the road.

"What're you doing?" Crow asked, glancing back over his shoulder at the car that had been following them.

"We need to settle this right here. I can't outrun them. Let's just get out of the car and do it, Crow." She pushed open the creaking driver's door and stepped out.

Crow hurried, doing the same. He said, "You take the keys?"

Heddy held up the car keys and shook them.

They both turned to face the oncoming headlights.

"Don't pull a gun until you know for sure," Heddy said. She had her hand in the green vinyl shoulder bag.

The car came toward them slowly. When it reached where they stood at the side of the road, it stopped. Crow stiffened. How damn many people had the meth crowd sent after them, a whole fucking battalion?

Someone got out on the driver's side and looked over the roof at them. "Got car trouble?"

He was about a hundred and fifty years old, Crow estimated. He had a white Santa Claus beard and enough wrinkles to rival the surface of the moon. This was not someone tailing them from the wreck, couldn't be. The tough guys in St. Louis didn't hire on geezers. The relief that flooded through Crow was like a whoosh of cool wind down a hot canyon wall.

"Nah, we're okay, Pops."

"Anything I can do to help?"

"Nope, thanks for stopping." Crow gave little thought to taking the old man's car. It was something from the forties, something almost as old as he was. A faded, black round-roofed car that looked like a hearse. They'd be no better off hijacking it.

When the old man pulled away, Crow gave Heddy a grin. "We're getting paranoid."

"*Getting?* I've already passed paranoid into insane." She laughed a little, relieved too.

Back in the car with the Escort on the highway again, Crow said, "They check out that Riviera, they're going to wonder where the owner is."

"I thought of that." Heddy looked over at Jay. "But I don't think we can let them go."

Crow wondered why. Yeah, they knew where he and Heddy were going, but what did it matter? They'd be out of the country before anyone caught them. Maybe. Maybe not. He wasn't sure about that, really. For that reason or perhaps reasons of her own, Heddy just didn't want to let the family go. For his part, Crow realized with a shock that he wouldn't be able to pull a trigger on Carrie or the little girl. He had a thing for Carrie. It's true she had talked him out of doing anything back in the motel room, but even that made him want her more. She spoke to him in a soft, soothing voice. She appealed to his honor and no one had done that in years. Relinquishing the idea of taking her against her will made him feel cleaner somehow than he'd felt in ages. He might be a lot of things, but rapist wasn't one of them.

Oh, he could do Jay easy, no problem, kill him dead, but kill a kid or a woman he wanted to fuck? Not in this life-time. So they'd have to let all three of them go.

He hadn't wanted to bust the woman in the woods, for that matter. He thought about it before he did it. He didn't listen to her. He'd heard better pleading from guys in Leavenworth. Shit, he'd done better begging *himself*. Not that it had saved him either. It just seemed sort of sad to murder a woman because she had driven her car down the wrong road at the wrong time. Wasteful. She was old, maybe forty-five, and she was fat as a butterball and she was, in the end, dead as sin, lying on her stomach in old dead leaves with a hole in her head. Damn shame.

He realized he was really turning into a stone killer, just what Jay Anderson said he was. When you can put down a woman like that, you have to have a stone for a heart.

He shrugged. No use getting in a panic over what was dead and done. No use at all.

He needed to get cranked. He'd felt pretty secure when they had the brand new Riviera and three hostages for cover if they got caught. But now, riding in this rustbucket, squeezed next to the little girl who had been silent the entire time, he felt like he was two steps away from a prison cell again. If he could crank up, maybe he'd stop worrying about it.

Hell, let Heddy do the worrying. That was her job anyway. If she happened to stay sober enough.

* * * * *

I think Heddy knew, even after she had stopped and found out the car following us wasn't after her, that they were back there behind us—the people from St. Louis. Daddy told Mama and me that Crow and Heddy must have knocked over a lab house, probably crack, a crack house, or meth, he said, a meth house, crank, he explained, worth a bundle on the street. That's what he said, *knocked over,* but I knew he meant they robbed it. I had seen crack houses on TV on cop shows. People involved in them were all members of the gangs and stuff, real gangsters.

Daddy had whispered to us about this while Heddy was out getting food for us and Crow went to the bathroom. Crow came out and Daddy didn't say anymore.

Now we had been in a wreck where I got thrown onto the floorboard behind the front seat, bumping my head and scraping my knees on the carpet. And because of Heddy, we'd just walked away. There were a lot of people, but they were all over the wrecked cars and didn't even notice when we left. It's amazing how people center in on a wreck, ignoring everything else.

Heddy took us up through the woods and came out on the road a long way in front of where the wreck happened. She made us stay in the woods until she went to the road and waved down a car. When she brought the driver to us, a really scared-looking woman in a flowered red dress who smelled like she'd been eating licorice whips, Heddy made us cross the ditch and get in the car.

It wasn't anything like my Daddy's car. It was little and we were all shoulder to shoulder in the back seat. I was practically sitting on Crow's lap. And the car made lots of noises and stunk pretty bad with the smoke coming out the rear end. You know how I've told you places and people sometimes have smells? Well, the old car they stole from that woman smelled of old things, really old, and poor things, like secondhand clothes they sell at garage sales.

Heddy cussed and carried on about it. She got mad

when Crow asked her why she took a car that bad.

The woman the car belonged to never came out of the woods. I hope she's all right. Did anyone find her? Did she get a ride? Well, it was better she stayed in the woods and wasn't made to go with us because it just got worse and worse with Crow and Heddy. At that time I didn't think it *could* get worse, but it did.

After we were on the road a while, not going very fast, Crow took another square from the tinfoil packet in his purse. He was right about me knowing what it was. I've never seen it up close or anything, but even in little towns kids do drugs, you know.

Not me. My Daddy would kill me if I ever did something like that. About once a week he told me how bad drugs were and if I ever saw kids doing them I was supposed to tell him. I couldn't do that, of course. They were just kids and if I told, they'd go to jail. Most of them knew my Daddy was a policeman so they didn't let me see much anyway.

After Crow put the drug up his nose, then rubbed the residue on his gums in his mouth, he went bonkers. He jiggled next to me like a little monkey. He started talking about crazy stuff, things that didn't make sense. Something about a guy called "Mod Squad" and about shivs made out of plastic tableware and fires in the bunks and closets where guys did the sex thing—although he used another word for it, one I'm not allowed to say.

He'd start talking about one thing and suddenly be talking about something else. I didn't want to hear what he was saying or what he was thinking. I stayed away from him, pushing up close to my Mama. I whispered to her, "Mama, can we ever go home?"

She hugged me and kissed me. I saw she was crying so I

didn't ask her anything else. She didn't know anymore than I did, really, even if she was grown-up and smart and a teacher. Maybe I even knew more because I could tell what people thought sometimes. It made me feel so alone. As much as my parents wanted to take care of me and protect me, they couldn't do a thing about the situation we were in.

Heddy got to the next town and found a motel that was dark and shabby. We never stayed in good places, like Best Westerns and Holiday Inns. We'd look funny going to our rooms the way Heddy and Crow were dressed, like street bums.

When we pulled up in front of the motel door, she had to shake Crow to wake him up. He'd talked himself straight into sleep. When he woke, he was real hateful and sassy, telling Heddy she had no right pushing him around, why didn't she just let him sleep in the car?

She didn't even offer to let us take a shower. I told her I was dirty and she just stared at me like I was crazy. I didn't tell her again. I knew that Crow did stuff without using his brain. He didn't even think about stuff. But Heddy thought it out and if she ever wanted to shoot me, if she got to thinking I was too much trouble, she'd do it in a pretty nasty, scary way. She'd let me see the gun and maybe feel it against my skin before she shot me.

Once that thought got in my head, I couldn't get it out. I couldn't go to sleep the rest of that night because of it. My stomach hurt, thinking about it. And I was hungry; I hadn't eaten much chicken.

But the worst thing was thinking about Heddy and what she'd do if she ever decided it was time to get rid of me. I must have shivered all night and finally shut my eyes when it was very late and maybe slept a little bit.

The next thing I knew, Heddy was coming through the

motel room door and slamming it behind her.

"That goddamn stinking torn-up rattletrap piece of shit won't start!"

"Hell." Crow came from the bathroom with a towel around his waist, his gun hanging from his hand. He'd just showered and he had untied Daddy to let him take a bath now. Mama was next and then me. I really needed a shower and I needed some clothes. We'd left our things in the Riviera. I guess we were going to have to put on our dirty clothes again. I'd never done that before, ever. Just the idea of it was nasty.

Heddy stomped around the bed and threw herself down on it so that she bounced and her feet left the floor. She was in a regular snit, like a little kid can get into sometimes, throwing herself around all dramatically the way she was.

"Now what do we do?" That was Crow, standing there looking hangdog and lost.

"Well, we don't call the Ford service center, that's for sure," she said.

Crow laughed until he saw her face. He cleared his throat. "Shit, we'll just take another car. No big deal."

"Great. Which one?"

"Huh?"

"Look out the window, Goof. We're the only people here. There *ain't* no cars out there."

Crow walked to the window and pulled up the dusty Venetian blinds. He turned back. "Now what?"

"I guess we're stuck here. Until someone else comes."

"That might not be until tonight."

"So we wait till tonight."

"What are we going to eat?"

Heddy gave him a withering look. "I think it's time *you* go out for the food. I've been doing every goddamn thing. I

112

drive the cars, I take the cars, I get the food, I get us out of tight spots like that wreck . . ."

"All right, all right, I get the message!" Crow turned his back, dropped the towel so his skinny white butt showed while he dragged on jeans and a shirt. He found his satchel and stormed out the door, slamming it behind him.

I sure hoped he wouldn't come back with hotdogs. Did I tell you I hate hotdogs now?

★ ★ ★ ★ ★

Hawkins remembered the day he decided to call up Jay's superior to find out where he was. It was one day after Jay's scheduled session. He knew the family had left for vacation, but they were to return two days before and Jay had arranged to be in Charlotte for therapy the following day. One thing Frank could always depend on with Jay Anderson was his punctuality. He never missed an appointment. He was never even late to one.

"Hey, this is Frank Hawkins down in Charlotte. Could you let me speak to Jay?"

"Jay's not back yet, sir." The sheriff's secretary knew everyone who worked from her office. "You want to talk to the sheriff?"

Frank, surprised to hear Jay hadn't returned, said yes. When he hung up from talking to the sheriff, he sat worrying a pencil stub between his teeth. Jay was two days late from vacation? Without calling?

The next day he got a call from the sheriff. The police in

Tarrant County had impounded Jay's new car down in Oklahoma.

"It's been in a wreck?"

"That's what they tell me. A godalmighty bad wreck too. They think it's totaled out."

"Did Jay mention he was going to Oklahoma?"

"No, see that's it. He said they were going over to Missouri and back. That doesn't include Oklahoma if my geography's any good."

"And he hasn't called?"

"Not only hasn't he called, but the impound place said the only way they knew who the car belonged to was the owner's papers in the pocket compartment. No one's showed up to claim the car since it was hauled away by wreckers."

Frank's anxiety deepened. "You checked the hospitals, I guess."

"Certainly. There's been no one admitted under the Anderson name."

"And . . . you checked the . . . morgue?"

"No dead Andersons either."

"How about if I go out there to check it out?" Frank asked.

The sheriff sounded relieved. "I'd sure 'ppreciate that, Frank. I can't leave and I don't have nobody else here I can do without either, not with Jay off work. But somebody's got to clear up the mystery of a wrecked vehicle and the missing family. If they're not dead from the wreck, why hasn't Jay called in? It's got me worried to death."

"Consider it done."

Frank got permission to make the flight and spend the days necessary to find the missing Anderson family. He rented a car and drove directly to the police impound lot.

"Mind if I snoop around the car?" he asked.

114

They gave him freedom to do whatever he wanted. Inside the wrecked car he found suitcases in the trunk with changes of clothes and toiletries for Jay, his wife, and daughter. Inside the car, he searched around and could find nothing that might give him a clue to their whereabouts. There were some gum papers on the backseat floorboard, that was about it.

He did find blood on the rear left passenger door. He called in forensics and the fingerprint team. Just the suggestion of foul play combined with the mystery of the missing family warranted further investigation.

Frank took a room in the town where the car was being held in impound. The morning after he'd called for an investigation, he received a phone call from a state lab.

"Frank Hawkins?"

"That's me. What did you find?"

"Something I know you—and the Feds—will be interested in."

"Yes?" Get on with it, he thought.

"The blood type matches the fingerprints lifted in the car for an escaped convict from Leavenworth, one Craig Walker. He busted out less than a week ago. The bulletins on him suggest he's traveling with a girlfriend with a sheet for felonies an arm long. She lived in St. Louis, Missouri until Craig broke out. They think she might have helped him escape the area, provided the car. They can tell you more, but that car of hers—not the Anderson car, but the car registered to the girlfriend?"

"Yeah?"

"It was found abandoned in woods not far from some tourist caverns in Missouri. This Craig character's been in other wheels since then. Evidently he was in Anderson's wheels."

Frank sat on the side of the motel bed and wondered what he could do besides alert the FBI an escaped convict had definitely crossed state lines and doubtless had a cop's family as hostage.

After making the necessary phone calls, he took the next flight for Kansas. He was heading for Leavenworth.

* * * * *

Crow found a music channel on the television and turned the volume full blast. He felt so antsy that he couldn't be still. When Heddy told him to turn it down, he ignored her. Fuck her. Fuck this shit. Hadn't he been the one to go for food? Hadn't *she* been the one to complain about how much she hated Mexican? Hadn't he done everything she'd told him for hours? Hadn't *she* not bothered, once, to say *thank you?* You'd think she'd show a little gratitude. Didn't she know how hard it was to walk down the streets out there while wondering if people were behind their shades and curtains, dialing the cops on him?

Since hitting the outside mere days ago he had had sex a few times, two Miller Lites, one T-bone steak (the first day he and Heddy skipped). It wasn't enough of the good life for someone who had been locked up in the slammer for four years, *taking orders, taking shit.* He felt like belting someone for all the years he had lost.

Those four years hadn't been the first time they'd stolen away his freedom. He'd been in and out of various institutions since he hit the streets at the age of ten goddamn years old—Emily's age. Life sucked. Life was about as much fun as having a pipe organ blow the strains of the *Star-Spangled Banner* up your ass.

He began jiggling around and then throwing himself into the heavy metal rock coming from the band gyrating on the television. He was sure glad they had cable and MTV. He threw his head front and back, flailed his arms, and bounced on the balls of his feet. If this music didn't cheer him up, he didn't know what he'd do, but it would be something bad.

"What's wrong with you, Crow, you sick?" Heddy yelled. "You got to play it that loud?"

He ignored her. Ignore, ignore, I don't know you, you bitch, he thought fiercely. I don't know no one. I don't need no one. I'm five seconds away from leaving this shithole with you in it.

To his surprise, Heddy came over to where he was moving like a madman and she began to dance too. She threw off the ugly curly wig and began flipping her head back and forth so that her long hair, still damp from a shower, came over her face and back again.

"Awwwright!" he screamed. "Gyrate, baby!"

Someone banged on the door. Crow yelled, "Go fuck yourself!"

Heddy stopped abruptly and turned down the TV. "Who's there?" she asked.

"Could y'all turn that noise down a little? You can hear it all the way out to the road."

Heddy must have recognized the dopey-looking motel clerk's voice. "You heard the man. FUCK OFF! I paid for this fucking room, so get lost!"

She whipped the volume up again and danced until they were both wet with sweat. Crow, incredibly aroused and not at all depressed anymore, got Heddy around the waist and threw her onto the empty second bed.

"Take out the kid."

Crow froze, for a moment thinking Heddy was telling him to kill the kid. Then he realized she meant "take the kid to the bathroom so we can fuck." He laughed wildly and bounded off the bed. He untied Emily's ankles and led her to the bathroom. She asked if she could sit on the toilet lid. He shrugged and let her, then closed the door. He whooped like crazy, sailed over the end of the bed where Jay and Carrie lay on their backs, bound and wordless, and landed on top of Heddy. She grunted, rolled him to the side, and started working the zipper of his jeans.

He felt like a hundred million. In ones! Heddy always did that for him.

The music channel changed programs and a soft-voiced girl sang about love, lost and regained. Perfect music for the scorched souls of a pair of lovers who needed a break, Crow thought, pushing into Heddy. Just perfect, man, this warm spot, this warm spot that cured the world's woes.

* * * * *

The hours spent in the motel stranded were the most normal any of us had seen. We took showers and even though we didn't have our suitcases any longer so we had no clean clothes, it was great to be under the showerhead, washing out the dirt of two days on the road.

I always liked taking a bath. A shower, really. Mama was

always getting onto me for standing under the warm water for over an hour, just dreaming. I couldn't take an hour bath in the motel, but just the same I felt a whole lot better afterwards.

Then Crow brought us back some Mexican food. Tacos and burritos and chili con questo. I even ate my guacamole salad because it was green and it tasted so fresh. I don't think anyone else ate the guacamole.

After we ate, Mama did the craziest thing. We were all untied so we could eat and close to the time we were all about finished, Mama stood up from the bed with her paper plate and walked toward the door. We all thought she was taking the plate to the trash can standing there, next to the TV, but she kept going, got her hand on the door knob, and just . . . sort of walked out.

She didn't even close the door all the way behind her. She just walked out!

Heddy was up and out the door after her before Crow even got his face out of his food long enough to notice she was gone.

I called, "Mama!"

Daddy stood up and dropped his paper plate and plastic fork, he was so shocked.

Heddy came back in, leading Mama by the arm, pinching her arm I think because Mama was making a face like it hurt. Then I remembered that was the arm she'd hurt in the wreck.

I said, "You're hurting my Mama. Let her go."

Heddy let her go, but after she'd slammed the door shut and locked it, putting on the safety chain, she turned around and gave me a look like, *You watch it, little girl.*

"Just what the hell did you think you were doing?" Heddy asked Mama.

Crow had stopped eating finally and he said, "She must be loco. From the food, huh? Loco, Mexican, you get it?"

Heddy didn't like joking when she was mad. "You think you can just walk out of here? Is that what you think?"

Mama had not said a word and she said nothing now. Daddy asked, "Are you all right?"

She nodded, but she wouldn't look at him.

I think maybe Mama got to a point, after all the stuff that'd happened, where she cracked a little—like an egg you're boiling. You leave it on the burner too long and the water burns out and then the egg cracks and sticks to the pan. She hadn't put up much protest through this whole thing, but maybe it was hurting her worse than either Daddy or me. Mama'd been through a lot and I didn't believe she was even thinking when she went through the door.

I could smell her unhappiness and the thought she had that there was no hope. It smelled like an old sofa pillow that everyone punches and puts beneath their heads and backs. Getting worn out, getting so old it needs to be thrown out.

Heddy and Crow didn't bother her anymore because maybe they knew she was doing harmless stuff. She wasn't threatening them. She was just a little lost, maybe even a little crazy.

I sat next to her on the bed and held her hand. She said, "I love you, Emily."

I said, "I love you too, Mama."

Crow said, "Oh give me a break with this love shit."

He was tying Daddy's hands again now that we were through eating.

The rest of the day was spent trying not to get on one another's nerves. The room was small, shabby, dark enough we had to keep the lamps on. Crow asked Daddy about the town where we live in North Carolina. At first Daddy didn't want to talk to him, but Heddy started asking him questions too and soon he was having a talk with them. Not like they were old friends, not like that, but he stopped sounding so angry after a little while.

"I've been a cop since I was twenty," he said.

"So, hey, what's it like busting the bad guys?" Heddy asked.

Daddy gave her a close look to see if she was baiting him. He said, "I just do my job."

"You think Crow ought to have wound up in Leavenworth for self-defense?"

Daddy laughed a little.

"What's so funny? She asked you a question." Crow had his back up, scowling like a bald-headed monkey waiting for a researcher to come with the needle.

"They all call it self-defense. What'd you do again, stab a guy in the stomach with a pool cue?"

"He pulled a knife on me first, said I was cheating."

"Were you?"

"What the hell difference it make, man? He had no call to pull the knife."

"I'm no judge," Daddy said, deliberately sidestepping the question.

"Well, you don't know nothing. You ever been broke? No place to stay the night?"

"I'm just about always broke."

"Right!" Crow barked out his disbelief. "You drive a Riviera, you're a cop, your wife's a teacher, and you're always broke. Right."

"After I make the payments on the car and the house and the credit cards, yeah, I am totally broke."

"It ain't the same, man. You don't know what it's like needing a meal. A crust of bread! You'd steal too if you were hungry."

"I'm sure I would. That why you took the money from the lab house? You were hungry?"

Crow narrowed his eyes. "What makes you so smart? How come you don't think I'll just pistol whip you to death one of these times you smart off like that?"

"You practically rape my wife, you terrify my daughter, you steal my car, you use me, and I'm going to be afraid of you? What else do I have to look forward to in the catalogue of terror tactics you have up your sleeve? After a while a person gets used to the way things stand, he gets immune. Or didn't you discover that yourself while in prison?"

"What's that supposed to mean? What're you getting at, man?"

"Don't talk to him, Crow." Heddy had drifted away from the two men and sat down in the desk chair. She'd been drinking from her bottle of whiskey, staring at the wall as if she could see a funny movie there. Half her mouth, the half that worked, smiled like she was having a great dream.

Mama lay down after a while and I still sat near, holding her hand. I'd done that before. When Daddy was mad at her or had hit her, she often took to bed and I sat with her, hoping she'd say something, anything, so I'd know she was going to be all right.

Just before dark Crow started acting weird, turning up some music on the TV real loud and dancing around like nobody I've ever seen dance. Then Heddy started dancing with him and, afterward, they got in the bed together. I had to sit in the bathroom and Crow let me sit on the toilet lid to wait. It was more comfortable than sitting on the floor. Not as cold, either.

I guess it's fair to say I don't like staying in bathrooms longer than I have to, not even for long showers. Not since being around those two.

* * * * *

No one stopped to take a room where we were staying. It wasn't exactly an inviting kind of stopover place. Finally, too anxious to stay off the road any longer, Heddy said we'd try to get the car started again. After Crow fiddled with something under the hood, it started. He hee-hawed like a madman. "Told you I could fix it!"

We were on our way again. It looked like Heddy would drive into the night so she could get farther south.

The worn out Ford Escort got us into the state of Texas before it died the next morning, shuddering and screaming like some kind of cat being skinned alive. Heddy pulled it over to the side of the road and we all just sat in the car, waiting.

It was the hottest time of day and we were all tired out, sleeping just a little through the night. The Escort rocked on its tires as cars whooshed past it. We were on Highway 83 South somewhere outside the town of Paducah, Texas in the upper panhandle where a big blue sky hung overhead, cloudless. Heat shimmered in violet waves off the pavement, making mirage puddles.

I looked at the back of Heddy's head and then at the back of my Daddy's head. I looked over at Crow. He sat quietly with his hands in his lap, staring at the back of Heddy's head too.

123

Were we just going to sit there with sweat crawling down our backs, alongside the road all day, I wondered?

The windows were down and the sounds of the passing cars filled our ears. *Whoosh. Whoosh.* I studied the drifts of wildflowers growing in the weeds that covered the ditch next to the road—Indian paintbrush, bluebonnets, and wild sunflowers nodding on tall stems that swayed every time a car passed. I'd read somewhere that Lady Bird Johnson, the former First Lady, had started the program to seed Texas highways with wildflowers. I thought that was a pretty cool idea. It made things pretty. But it didn't stop the heat.

After a long while Heddy moved. She leaned forward in the seat and tried the ignition. The starter on the car whined. She kept trying. Finally the car caught life and suddenly Crow let out a whoop that made me jump.

"Goddamn, I thought we were done for this time!"

Heddy pumped the gas to keep the car going, but it coughed smoke and still shuddered like it was sick. She said, "It might get us to the next town. That's all it's got to do."

She put on her turn signal and watched for a break in the traffic on the inside lane before pulling out slowly. Cars had to go around us. We couldn't have been traveling faster than thirty miles an hour all the way to the next little place that was called Guthrie, Texas. The car lurched and growled and smoked. I caught myself wishing it would make it. I didn't know what Heddy might do if it broke down there on the highway where a cop car might stop to check on us.

Heddy pulled the Escort into the parking lot of a PiggyWiggly store and let the old car finally die.

"Now what?" Crow asked.

"We need another set of wheels."

"Well, I *know* that."

"Then why'd you ask?" Heddy looked over her shoulder at him as if he were nuts.

"I'm going in the store for some food." Crow climbed out of the car and stretched. "I ain't sitting in this baking oven another second."

"I have to go to the bathroom," I said. "Heddy? Can I?"

"Not yet." She was staring out the windshield, studying the parking lot.

"But I have to go to the . . ."

"Shut up!"

A blue van with silver stripes pulled into the entrance and moved past us slowly like a big ship gliding past, blocking the sky.

"That's what we're taking," Heddy said, getting out of the car. "Come on, get out and walk in front of me."

We all got out of the car. Daddy said, "You're going to take that van? In broad daylight?"

"Watch me," she said, pushing him across the lot toward the van. "You ought to have a little more confidence. I could teach you how to be a pretty good car thief if you'd pay attention."

"I don't think car theft is in my stars," Daddy said.

It was tall and blue and square, like a bus, with silver stripes down the center of the sides. By the time it was parked, Heddy had us at the side door that faced away from the store. Her gun was out and in her hand. The door opened and out stepped a young man wearing suspenders over a pinstriped shirt with a pair of blue slacks. He looked startled to find so many people that near to his vehicle.

"Hello," Heddy said. "Mind if we see what this baby looks like inside?"

She let the man see the gun and he moved out of the

way, his hands going up a little. "Put your hands down, stupid." Heddy leaned over the driver's seat and looked around. "How's the gas mileage on a thing like this?"

The man blinked. "Uh, it's not bad," he said. When Heddy waited, staring at him he added, "Maybe eighteen to a gallon, open road."

"Good," Heddy said. "Give me the keys and get in the back with the others."

I could see Crow coming across the lot through the window of the van. He was headed for the Escort. Heddy saw him too. She said, "Open that window." The man did as he was told and Heddy yelled out, "Crow! In here!"

Crow halted and stared incredulously at the new shiny van, then he grinned like a crazed overheated dog that's found a patch of shade. He ambled over to the vehicle, circled it, opened the door, and came inside. He had a bag of groceries in his arms. "Hey, now this is using your noggin. What a set-up. Plenty of room for everyone." He twisted in the front seat and admired the double row of seats we sat on and the sofa in the very back.

Not far outside of Guthrie, Heddy took a right turn on a little used farm road and drove down it until she saw an opening on the site where a house used to stand. Wild orange and black speckled irises broke over the top of tall green grass, like colorful birds rising into the air. She pulled into the overgrown yard and parked the van, but left it idling.

She nodded her head at Crow. He said, "Come on, man, this is your getting-off place. We'll take real good care of your rig for you."

The man heaved a sigh of relief as he crawled from the seat next to us. He had tried to find out what his abductors were doing, why they'd brought him along, but couldn't get any information. He got out of the van and was almost smiling at the thought of being away from us. Crow followed him out.

I put my hands over my ears and then over my eyes. I felt Mama put her arm around my shoulder. We all knew what was going to happen and there was nothing we could do about it.

There were two shots, one after the other. Daddy said, "He's a damn man-eating shark. The man would kill anything."

"Yeah, I know," Heddy said. "Ain't we lucky?"

"You're closing the door on your own cellblock, Heddy."

Heddy sneered at him with her half-working mouth and said, "That's the by-God truth and don't forget it. As long as it's *my* cellblock and *I'm* the one closing the door, it's not your goddamn business." Suddenly she reached out and stroked Daddy's cheek. He flinched, as if she were about to hit him, but when she just stroked, he seemed to loosen, and then he smiled at her in a soft way I'd seen him smile at Mama before.

I looked at Mama, but she wouldn't look back. She had seen it, what passed between Heddy and Daddy, but she wasn't going to let me know what she thought.

Crow was back inside, telling Daddy to get out and get in the front. They switched places. Heddy turned the van around in the tall green swaying grass, crushing the orange irises beneath the wheels. She headed to the highway again.

Texas lay before us like a big, flat, desert place shimmering beneath the red sun. It was the first time that I thought maybe we weren't going to get out of this alive. Not any of us.

* * * * *

Heddy was a good driver, better than Crow could ever be, he realized, watching how she maneuvered the extra-long van down the highway. While she drove, he inspected the place. It was luxurious, almost a home on wheels. There was a color TV inset at the roofline just behind the front bucket seats. There were headphones on each side of the wide seats that he assumed worked off the stereo system. There were even recessed cup holders for drinks on each side of the bench seat.

He switched on the TV with the remote control, but the station kept fading out so that he turned it off again.

"Try the radio," he told Heddy and music spilled from invisible speakers in the doors and ceiling.

"This is one luxury vehicle," he said, taking an apple from the bag of groceries he'd bought. "Won't nobody suspect we're in something like this."

"We'll ditch it when we get to the border," Heddy said. "Maybe we'll walk across and buy something to drive in Mexico."

Crow crunched down on the apple and grinned over at the silent family. "This beats your Riviera all to shit," he said around the mouth full of apple flesh.

"Yeah, but it won't outrun a patrol car." Jay gave him a knowing glance.

"It won't have to. There's not one after us. So why don't you give it a rest?"

Jay shrugged.

Emily said, "I need to go to the bathroom."

"I'll stop somewhere in a little while," Heddy said.

"Even you couldn't afford something like this," Crow said to Jay. "Come to think of it, the guy we left back in those weeds couldn't afford it for very long."

"It cost him his life, didn't it?" Jay asked. "You're just a lowlife killer, aren't you? That makes you a big man, doesn't it? With that gun, you're the Pope and the President all rolled up in one little package, you rule the world."

"You got that right, motherfucker." Crow tossed the core of the apple on the floorboard and glared at Jay.

"Shut up, Jay," Heddy called from the driver's seat.

"And what if I don't? Going to kill me? Why don't you go ahead and get it the hell over with?"

Carrie said, "Please, Jay, don't."

"We're not going down into Mexico with you, I know that. You're either going to let us go or kill us all. Why not get it done now?"

"You got your pig face showing," Crow said. "And I'll smash it in for you if you keep it up."

"I'll pull this bastard over right here!" Heddy screamed, rooting everyone for a moment as she applied the brakes enough to cause Jay to grab hold of the dash.

"Daddy?"

Jay turned enough to see his daughter. It was as if she carried his sanity on her shoulders and when he saw her, it was returned to him. He slumped, settling into the bucket seat, his head hanging.

Suddenly Carrie squared her shoulders and began to talk in a firm voice. "Yes," she said, "my husband beats me and I have put up with it."

Jay swiveled his head to stare at her. He couldn't have looked more surprised if his wife had just said he drank camel piss and ate babies for lunch. Emily scooted close to her side and held onto her hand for support. The van picked up speed again, Heddy ignoring them once more.

"Go on," Crow said, "tell the truth, woman."

Carrie took a deep breath, but she would not look at her husband. She stared at her hands. "I didn't know he was that way when I married him. I'd known him in high school when he was the star quarterback and all the girls were crazy about him. It was all very romantic, the way he cared only for me. He bought me flowers, gave me his ring. It seemed right at the time when he got angry if any other boy asked me out. It's how all the boys acted, jealous and protective.

"But that first year of marriage after I'd finished getting my teacher's certificate and he hit me—I should have left him then. But I was . . . I was pregnant." She raised her head and looked sadly at Emily. "I didn't want to leave him. I thought it would get better."

"You've said enough," Jay said.

"She hasn't even fucking started," Crow said. "Go on, Carrie."

"I know now that I let him maim my spirit. He broke me as surely as someone breaks a wild horse. I'm guilty of letting that happen, of staying when I didn't have the strength to leave, of forcing my only child to watch the death of a marriage and the slow dying of the small love that was once between her parents."

"Oh Mama . . ."

Carrie patted her daughter's hand before continuing. "When the two of you found us, I'd determined to leave him. When we returned from our vacation, Emily and I were going away."

"It's none of their business," Jay said.

"Yes, it is. Yes, it's their business now because we're their business, Jay. They have the power to kill us or let us go. They need to know how much suffering we've already done when they make that kind of decision."

"Confession's good for the soul." Crow grinned in a lopsided way at Jay. "Let her tell it."

"I've heard it all before," Heddy said from the front. "Get out the violins. Abused women, big fucking deal."

Carrie burst into tears. She let the tears spill down her face without wiping them away. "I know it's a stupid life. It's the same life a million other women are living or have lived and I let myself become just another stupid statistic, a battered woman, a victim . . . a nobody. It's my fault, too. I let it happen, I stayed too long, I took it."

"It's not true, Mama." Emily squeezed her mother's hand and pushed her head onto her shoulder. "You stayed for me."

"But if you kill him, that doesn't clean the slate." Carrie turned her face to Crow. She looked past her husband to the violent and cruel man who had defended her once in the hotel room, the man who listened to her and was talked out of the idea of rape. "If you kill him, I don't get to leave him, do I? I don't get to fix all the wrong. I don't get to prove to my daughter that her mother is strong and can make a difference in her life."

Crow shrugged. "I don't know about all that." He seemed to think it over, watching her.

"Why don't you let us go now?" Carrie asked in a soft, pleading voice. "Let us finish our lives, let me have the chance to do the right thing."

"You ever leave me, I'll kill you."

Crow's eyes flicked from Carrie to Jay, then darkened. "I think he means it."

131

"Then he'll just have to kill me."

"That ain't gonna happen," Crow said. He pointed at Jay. "You just signed your death warrant, buddy. This woman needs you like she needs terminal cancer."

Jay stared out the side window.

Carrie wiped her face clear. She said, "You still won't let us go, will you?"

"No."

"You're going to kill us then?"

Crow didn't answer. The voice that answered came from the driver's seat when Heddy said, "He might not, but you can count on me."

Emily started to cry, her shoulders heaving. "It's all right," Carrie said. "Don't cry, baby, it's going to be all right no matter what happens."

You might think I shouldn't love my father for what he's done to my mother. The funny thing is I can love part of him and hate the other part. The part that is my father who rode me on his shoulders at the Thanksgiving Parade, the part that took me into Clarissa's Toy Shop downtown and bought me the prettiest porcelain doll they had for sale, the part that beamed over my report card grades— that's the part I love.

People, even parents, don't come all in a box with a bow tied around it, like a present—pretty and new and something you always wanted. They're made up of pieces and bits, some of it smooth like jewels shining and some of it jagged glass that can cut your heart out. You have to love what you can and stay away from the rest.

The one thing I couldn't forgive him for is when he said he'd kill Mama if she tried to leave him.

The one thing that surprised me about my Mama was how she didn't care. She said she'd go anyway. For the first time in our lives she was ready to stand up to him even if he threatened to take her life for it.

Maybe it was all these days under the strain and the fear with Heddy and Crow. It was also probably because she saw how Heddy touched Daddy and how he responded to her. That one sudden touch and the smile from it caused my mother to break out and say what she had to say, to face what she had to face. She had loved my father once and now she had to get away from him. She said it was to prove to me she could do it, but the truth was it was something she had to do to save herself.

When Heddy told us she would be the one to kill us, I knew it was the truth too. Heddy didn't say anything she didn't mean. I could tell by watching Crow as he listened to my Mama that he would never hurt her in any way. He was a killer, he'd already killed people in front of us, but my mother had found one of those jeweled parts in him and he'd never find his dead broken glass soul to cut her out of his life.

It seemed to me then that things were getting really complicated. Over three days and two nights Heddy and my Daddy were interested in one another. And Crow was interested in my mother, though she was older than he was. It made me dizzy to think of it. It made me nervous. I didn't know people could start, well, liking one another that way so fast.

Even though I knew now that Crow wouldn't want to hurt Mama, Heddy so far had not shown me any part of her that wasn't broken. It was like she was a shattered mirror and every piece of it had a crack from top to bottom, from side to side. If anyone could murder us, she could, and it wouldn't bother her a bit. But would Crow let her do that after what I saw in his eyes for my mother? Where would his loyalty lie in the end? He always did what Heddy said, but when it came to putting a bullet in me or my mother, would Crow let that happen?

I didn't know which one of them would win out in that contest. Heddy was the strongest, but maybe Crow hadn't been tested properly yet.

It was odd to hope that this man, this killer, would be the one to save us. But it was all we had.

The new van they'd stolen rolled down the highway across Texas. Outside the windows lay desert land, cacti, and little dusty towns that dozed like old shaggy cats lying spread out in the sun.

Daddy stayed completely still in his seat staring out the window, saying nothing. Crow watched everyone carefully. He made my skin crawl the way he watched us.

I daydreamed a little, remembering our house, the sidewalk in front of it, the street with the trees growing down each side shading the walk. I played there. It was where I learned to ride a bike and to skate. I had friends when I was little. We played games in the front yard and built Kool-Aid stands to sell cups of lemonade on summer days. But when I got older, around nine, I started to realize my friends wouldn't like it inside my house where there was so much silence and unhappiness. If you walked into our house from outside, you'd feel a chill. It wasn't natural in our house. It was like a freezer and we were all frozen in our places.

I stopped inviting friends over and they stopped inviting me to their houses until finally I had no friends left at all. It was better that way, just the three of us in the house alone, keeping the secrets.

I used to sit in my room and stare out the front window at the street thinking what I would be when I grew up and I could get away from my parents and the sadness they shared. I would be good, mostly. I would never be mean to another single person, never make anyone cry, never raise my hand to another. It's the lesson I'd learned and maybe the only one. It got to the point that I couldn't even harm an insect, couldn't swat at a fly on my arm or mash a big black ant if it crawled up my leg.

The horror of what I'd seen Crow and Heddy do was a hundred times worse than what my father did when he raised his hand to my mother, but in some ways not really any worse. They killed quickly, taking life in a flash. Daddy had been killing Mama slowly all of my life and longer, years of cutting away her love until she was half dead before she could manage to say she'd take it no more.

I'd sit on her bed and place a wet folded washcloth over her black eyes and ask her to talk to me, but she couldn't. She was too empty inside to tell me she was going to recover. Yet by the morning, she'd rise, wash her face, apply the thick pancake make-up and the tinted glasses, and she would go to school with me where she taught and I attended my classes. She'd do what she had to do, I guess, when she had to do it.

No one ever questioned us. Not me or Mama. Daddy was on the town's police force, what could they say? Maybe they were afraid he'd arrest them. For whatever reason the principal, Mr. Haddway, never called me in and he never asked Mama if she was going to be all right, if she needed help, if he could be of assistance.

It was as if only the kids were the honest ones. They whispered about the black eyes and bruises. They kept away from me so that I ate alone in the cafeteria and was never picked for any side in the games during gym.

I always thought that was for the best because I couldn't tell them why things were this way or how they would ever end. I never wanted to talk about it. Everyone else had a best friend. I didn't want any best friends because you had to tell them everything and I couldn't, just couldn't.

Toward evening the first day we were in the stolen van Crow started talking after he had some of the drug in his purse. He swiveled toward us and said, "I've got a whole lot of money here." He patted his leather bag. Patted it, patted it like a puppy.

Heddy heard him and warned, "Crow . . ."

He flipped his hand at her as if to say go away, you bother me, then continued. "I haven't counted it, but it's a lot of money, more money than your ole man's ever made in his entire life. What do you think of that?"

Mama said, "It might get you killed."

Crow laughed. "Likely as not, unless we get across that border before they catch up with us." He turned and looked out the square back windows. "I don't know who's back there. They might be back there, all right."

"Why don't you shut up, Crow? Damn. Do not. Do you hear me? Do not get paranoid on me."

Again he ignored Heddy's command. "With this kinda money, I can buy a castle in Mexico. One on a hilltop by the ocean, maybe, and hire me a bunch of Mexicans to wait on me hand and foot. We could all go on down there and live like kings . . . except for *him*." He pointed a bony finger at the back of Daddy's head.

Mama just blinked hard and looked sad. Outside dark fell and the headlights of oncoming cars tracked against the tinted glass like wild eyes striking the curved glass and sliding off into darkness. I think Mama knew like I did that Heddy wouldn't let him kill my Daddy and not us. She'd never let us live in a castle on the beach with Crow. It was all a pipe dream, a fairy story. Only we were all the Three Little Pigs and Heddy was the wolf. The Big Bad Wolf, ready to huff and to puff and to blow our house down.

* * * * *

Maybe it was because Carrie finally said and did what his own mother never had the guts to say or do that Crow came to have his feelings for her. Her determination combined with her fragile demeanor and frail looks, made her heroic in his eyes. In his whole life he'd never held up anyone as a hero. Through the juvenile halls and foster care system he'd only run into shits, real shits. People out to use, abuse, and confuse him. Old story, a really depressingly familiar old story, one he knew wasn't much different from a million other stories he'd heard while in the joint.

His own mother, for not standing up for herself against his two-fisted shit of a father, had paid the ultimate price. The brain damage they discovered in her last hospitalization left her without her own name, much less her son's. She was put into a place where she never came out again, dying senseless and alone.

Crow never went to see her, even after he was on the

street and free. He didn't want to look again on her empty eyes and watch the slobber dribble down her chin. If he had to see that again, he'd go up like dynamite and kill every motherfucker in sight.

It's what made him hate Jay with a passion you don't generally hold for a stranger. It became more and more clear to him that he might be Carrie's savior by being Jay's executioner. She might never forgive him for it, and the kid would never forget her father had been murdered at his hands, but, nevertheless, he would have put one son of a bitch out of this world who needed it and there was something to be said for that. The problem with the plan was that something was cooking in Heddy's brain about the guy. He knew when she liked a guy, and she liked this one. She took more shit off him than she should have; she wouldn't let him go even when she had a chance and should have. Could it be that she was stuck on him the way he was getting stuck on Carrie? It was like he and Heddy were tripping over themselves to find new bed partners. Straight ones. Square ones.

It was turning into a hell of a mess, so tangled he couldn't get it undone.

Heddy pulled the van into the deserted gravel parking lot of a country stockyard outside the city limits of Abilene, Texas. The sun had been down for a couple of hours and the wind-washed town of Abilene blinked with oil refinery lights to the north of them.

Crow could smell the creosote-soaked timbers and the rotten-egg stink of oil derricks. He could hear in the background the steady *thump-thump* of the drilling rigs pumping black gold from the bowels of the earth.

"I wonder why anyone lives way the hell out here," he said. It gave him the heebie-jeebies. He shivered all over with a chill.

Heddy asked, "What did you buy at the store?" He showed her the lunchmeat and bread and cheese. She told Carrie, "Make sandwiches."

Crow didn't think Heddy was acting right, not like herself, but he wasn't sure what was wrong. She left the driver's seat and told him to get in the back, let her sit down. He did as she said, bouncing a little on the sofa in the back. He watched as she turned on the TV with the remote and scanned both channels that came in clear enough to see before settling on "Jeopardy." She hadn't looked him in the eye once.

"What burr got up your ass?" he asked.

"I've been watching you in the mirror," she said.

"What's that supposed to mean?"

"I've seen how you look at her."

Crow glanced over at Carrie making the sandwiches. The little girl was helping her. Both of them were assiduously ignoring the conversation. In the front seat Jay still sat unmoving and silent. At least he knew his place—which was outside the pale.

"What's your point, Heddy?" He never figured her for jealousy. Hadn't she screwed Jay? Right in front of him? And did *he* get his britches in a bunch over it? Hell no! There wasn't any room between them for being jealous. It was an emotion neither of them had kept around for very long. He no more owned a piece of Heddy than he could own the moons of Jupiter.

"I say we dump 'em here. When we take off in the morning, we go alone."

Crow hawked out a laugh. "Yeah, and before we hit the border, we have a thousand cop cars surrounding this boat. That makes perfect sense, Heddy. We've come this far . . ."

"You're not taking her with us!" Heddy was off the bench seat, turning, and throwing the remote control at his face. He ducked in time before it struck him, his mouth hanging open at her sudden vehemence.

"Hey, take it easy . . ."

"We should have dumped them in the beginning. We never should have brought them along!"

"Well, it's a little late for that. And it was *your* fucking idea, remember?"

"It's not too late now. I don't want them with us anymore."

"And what if I do?"

Heddy grabbed her green vinyl bag from the floor next to the driver's seat and flung herself at the handle of the sliding side door. She went out, slamming it behind her. The van rocked.

Crow twisted on the sofa to watch her through the window. She stomped away toward the corrals of the stockyard. She climbed the board fence and sat on top, staring out across the trodden ground to the big hulking warehouse where trucks brought in livestock when there was a public sale.

Crow muttered, watching her, "Crazy bitch."

"Do what she says," Carrie said.

Crow said, "You'd like that, wouldn't you? We put you all out here and you flag down the next patrolman to point out we're traveling in this fancy van on our way to Mexico."

She shook her head. "We don't have to tell anyone anything."

"And what about *him?* You think he'll keep quiet?"

Carrie looked away and took more bread from the package. "You could tie him up. You could . . . you could even knock him out." After she'd said it, she seemed shocked at herself.

"Oh, that's real nice, Carrie," Jay said from the front. "I want to thank you for that."

Crow looked outside again, wondering if Heddy would

go for it, if maybe that wouldn't be the wisest move, and saw a car turning into the stockyard.

"It's a cop," he said, hurriedly shuffling through his leather bag for his gun.

"I hope he blows your eyes out," Jay said.

Crow rose, went to the door and stood hunched over before it, watching through the window there. The car drove close to the van and stopped. A cop in full uniform, all tan and black, got out of the patrol car, hitching his pants up by his belt. He looked over the van from front to back before approaching the door. Crow said quietly, "You say anything, I kill the bastard."

Deeper night darkness had swept in even as Crow had been talking to Carrie so that now he couldn't even see the fence of the stockyard where Heddy had gone to perch. He felt sweat break out under his arms and the smile plastered on his lips felt like a smear of glue across the lower half of his face. He took one step down and reached out to open the sliding door just before the cop went up to the passenger's seat to talk to Jay.

The door slid open noisily. He stood looking down at a young man with green smiling eyes.

"Howdy, folks. Thought I'd stop to see if you're having any trouble. This is private property and I'm afraid you can't stay here." He peered past Crow's body to the woman and child making sandwiches.

Crow had his gun behind him. He said, "I'm sorry, officer, we didn't mean to break any laws. Our engine was running hot so we just pulled over for a little while. We'll be on our way in a few minutes."

"Would you mind stepping out so we can talk, sir?" the cop asked. "Bring along registration and your insurance card, if you don't mind." He was still smiling, being sociable, but behind his friendly words camped pure steel. If everything was as it seemed, it was going to be all right. If it was hinky, they were going to be in trouble—that's what his voice promised.

Crow saw only the flicker of a shadow behind the policeman before the flash and the blast caught the intruder in the back. The cop stood one moment facing Crow, shock entering his smiling eyes, before he crumpled forward, his head hitting and clanging off the chrome running board before striking the ground.

Heddy stood silhouetted from the light spilling out the door, the gun dangling at her side. She said, "We have to get out of here."

"Christ, Heddy, you could have waited a minute, I think he believed me."

"Oh, fuck, just get back inside and get outta my way." She crawled up the steps and brushed past him to the driver's seat to start the van. "You don't know a goddamn thing."

Crow glanced once more at the body lying on the ground before closing the door and locking it against the night. "God, I wish that cop hadn't come here. I wish it wasn't so far across Texas," he said to no one in particular. "Mexico seems two million miles away."

By the time Heddy stopped at a service station for gas and let me go to the bathroom, I thought I'd bust. She came into the bathroom before I was finished, and stood in front of the sink mirror, drinking whiskey. She actually growled at me when I came out of the toilet so I didn't even try to wash my hands. I just wanted out of the room with her before she decided to use her gun on me.

Have you ever seen anyone stare at you like you're a nasty bug? That's how Heddy looked at me all the time. Like she wanted to crush me and walk on.

"Go straight to the van," she said, giving me that Wish I Could Stomp You Dead look.

I shut the door to the bathroom and heard her lock it. For some reason I stood there a minute, listening. That's when I heard her thoughts so loud they were like cymbals crashing. I put my hands over my ears, to block it out, but that didn't help. I started backing away from the door, horrified.

Heddy didn't have thoughts like other people. She didn't even have thoughts like Crow did when he was messed up on dope. I can't even tell you what exactly the thoughts were, they were too mixed up and crazy, but if thoughts were colors, hers would have been blood red. Like the fury of a whirlwind coming down out of the sky with chariots on fire in them. Like Satan riding a giant horse down over a city and knocking apart all the buildings like they were stacked dominoes.

She hated herself so much that the hate spilled over onto everything. Onto me, Crow, her life, and everything in it. I'd never known anyone who hated that much. Or anyone who scared me more.

I didn't even know what I was doing. I started running away from the locked bathroom door just to get away from her. Before I knew what I'd done, I was across the service station parking area and then across the broken pavement of an alley and then I was in the middle of someone's yard yelling, calling, crying, begging for help, hoping someone, anyone, would rescue me.

I didn't see Crow coming. He must have seen me take off because he caught me up by the waist and threw me over his shoulder, loping back across the alley and the parking lot and to the van. He threw me inside the open sliding door so that I landed on the floor, crying.

Mama reached down and took me into her arms. I had wanted to get away, just get away from Heddy and never come back. I didn't care, when I ran, what happened to my mother and father anymore. All I wanted to do was run and find help, any kind of help from anybody, but there was no one in that alley and no one in the house where I stood screaming in the night. The house was empty, deserted, and dark, and no one paid attention to a kid yelling her head off before Crow caught me and took me back.

"Don't pull a stunt like that again," Crow warned. He was all out of breath and sounded scared himself. He got inside and slammed the door shut.

No one said anything else while I cried and Mama brushed her hand over my hair.

I couldn't tell them what had scared me so. They wouldn't have believed me anyway. Mama knows I know things I shouldn't, but she doesn't really understand how I do it. She just thinks I'm sensitive and observant and that I pick up on things because I watch grown-ups and I pay attention. I'm *perceptive,* she'd say, using a teacher word.

How could I tell them that Heddy's brain was torn up and more crooked than her mouth? That she was mad as a coyote beneath a bad moon? That her head was full of chaos and death and blood and darkness so deep that it was swallowing her?

Crow couldn't even know what was in her head. If he

did, he would have run away with me and screamed for help just as I did. Or killed her. Crow should have killed her and stopped her misery, but he didn't know about it. No one knew but me.

I don't know where people get their problems from or how they live with them once they get that messed up in their heads. Looking at Heddy, how she drove the cars and how she never said much, you'd think she was a normal criminal—a woman heading for Mexico with her lover and however much money they had stolen from St. Louis. But that's not what Heddy was about at all.

She hated herself so hard that she was like a walking hole in the world. She was like a door into some other awful place where demons lived.

Not that I believe in demons and stuff. I used to go to the Baptist church with Mama and I couldn't quite believe some of those stories about Hell and the devil or even Heaven and God. Those are very big stories, you know, big and hard to believe.

All I knew, tapping into Heddy's thoughts, was that real Hell was inside people's heads and it was worse than what the Bible said about it. Worse than a lake of fire and brimstone.

No wonder Heddy drank all the time. It was the only way she kept from stepping out in front of a truck speeding down the street.

I would have been sorry for her if I hadn't been so scared.

When she came back to the van, I turned my face into Mama's stomach and kept my eyes shut tight. I locked her out. Locked out Heddy's mind and hoped I never stumbled onto the opening to it again.

I'd tell you more about what it was like, but I can't talk

about it. Just believe me. Heddy was the one we had to watch from now on. Crow didn't feel any regret when he had to kill people to steal their cars or steal their money, but he was like a cleaning machine that swept the streets. It was nothing to him, meant nothing at all.

For Heddy, killing was personal and it was something she liked, once she started doing it. When she did it, she did it like someone with a job she enjoyed. It was a pleasurable thing because if she didn't kill other people, she'd kill herself.

That made her our real enemy and the only one we had to worry about. If she'd been an illness, she would have been a real slow painful one where your skin and muscles fell off your bones while you watched, unable to believe it was so.

I was afraid we'd never get away from Heddy.

* * * * *

Frank walked through the corridors of Leavenworth, a security officer unlocking and re-locking doors behind them as they made their way to a room where one of the recaptured escaped inmates waited.

Frank remembered his impatience as he entered the room and took a chair at a scarred blue table with the prisoner. He realized the Anderson family must be hostages of Craig Walker, but they would never know where the family had been taken unless they discovered where Walker was headed. The FBI was dispatching someone soon to the prison to question the inmates, the same as Frank was doing. He just got to them first.

The initial three briefings with the returned prisoners didn't give Frank anything to go on. They claimed the escapees hadn't told one another of their plans for the outside. That way if one was caught, he couldn't squeal on someone else.

Frank almost believed that. Almost. But he had to keep questioning, because if he didn't get a lead that meant Jay, Carrie, and Emily were on their own somewhere no one could ever find them.

On the fourth inmate interview, Frank got a break. Charlie Holland had been caught two days after the escape. He had been roomed in a cell next to Craig Walker for eight months before the breakout.

Frank approached him in a different way than he had the others. He said, "Look, we believe Craig's taken a family hostage. There's a little girl involved, ten years old." He paused. "You have kids, Charlie?"

Charlie squirmed in his hard chair. He finally said, "Yeah, I do."

"How many? What's their ages?"

"What's the difference, man?"

"Just answer me, okay?"

"Two, girl and boy. Seven and five, Janine and Patrick."

"Then you know what you'd feel like if your kid had been kidnapped. Would you want your girl or boy on a joyride with Walker?"

Charlie shrugged, but there was worry on his face. He looked as if he were having trouble with the idea of it.

"Tell me where Walker was headed. I know he told you. Or you know something. We just want to get the family free and the little girl out of this safely."

"He didn't tell me nothin."

Frank lit a cigarette, offered the pack to the prisoner. Charlie took one and Frank put the Bic lighter flame to it. They sat smoking for a couple of minutes. Frank said nothing, giving Charlie time and space to think it over.

Charlie said finally, "I don't know what you want from me. I didn't take no kid."

"I want to save the little girl, Charlie. And her mother and father too. Maybe you overheard something, maybe you noticed something. If Walker didn't tell you . . ."

Charlie dragged deeply on the cigarette. As he exhaled he said, "Craig was hanging around the Spics before we broke out."

Frank leaned forward. "Why was he doing that?"

"I think he was trying to pick up a little Spanish."

Frank leaned back. "He was going to Mexico?"

Charlie shrugged again, blowing out the last of the smoke from his lungs. He took another drag. "Can I have the pack?" he asked.

Frank handed it over. Charlie put the pack into his pants pocket. "Hey, thanks."

"You know anything else might help me, Charlie?"

Charlie looked at the locked door behind Frank as he said, "Craig's girlfriend?"

"Yeah. We know about how she helped him by having a car waiting."

"I think she wanted him to go to St. Louis when he got out. See a guy named Rory or go where this guy worked with some people, some kinda shit like that."

"You have a last name, an address?"

"I think Craig mentioned 'Prairie.' Maybe that was a street or a suburb, hell, I don't know. When he was talking about going there, I told him he was crazy, man. He needed

148

to head south right off, soon as he got out. He said he needed a stash and this friend of his girl's was gonna help them out."

Frank took that information and left for St. Louis, Missouri the same afternoon. He was on Walker's old trail, trying to pick up a scent. All the time in the flight to the city and the drive in the rental car to police headquarters, he kept Jay's daughter and her welfare in the forefront of his mind. He hoped he wasn't going to be too late.

At least the blood in the Riviera belonged to Walker, not one of the Andersons. They must not have been hurt badly.

But where were they now? How could they walk away from a huge pile-up and traffic snarl and disappear?

When he got to St. Louis he heard about the dead woman, found shot to death alongside the road leading away from the accident scene.

Before Emily told him about the taking of the woman's Escort, he had known that part of the story. And that's nearly all he knew. It was much later before a report turned up on the dead owner of the blue van and the old red Escort was found abandoned in the parking lot of a PigglyWiggly store.

Highway 83 turned into Highway 84 outside of Abilene. At a little place called Coleman it changed again to Highway 283. But it was a tiny farm road, 783, that took them into Fredericksburg, Texas, a German-settled town smack in the heart of the rolling hill country. This is where a series of happenstances led Heddy and Crow into the arms of their outlaw enemies who had tracked them so diligently across country from St. Louis.

It was morning, hot already, a real I'm-Dying-Here Texas scorcher. The sun filled the sky, a disk of liquid gold dripping out of a blue palette, frying the pancake that was the earth.

The need for sweets and anything chocolate drove Heddy into stopping at a little convenience store just inside the city limits of Fredericksburg. She told Crow to pick up M&Ms, Almond Joys, and cartons of chocolate milk while she stayed in the van and watched the passengers.

Just as Crow brought an armload of these items to the counter, the thirteen-inch black-and-white television playing behind the male clerk ran a newsbreak special about the escaped convicts from Leavenworth, two of whom were still on the loose. Crow stood rooted to the spot, staring at his ugly, longhaired mugshot filling the small screen. "Well, fuck."

The employee, a short man with a dark widow's peak and a Fu Mann Chu mustache, noticed his customer's stare, turned, and saw the same thing. When he turned back, his right sneakered foot was already inching close to the button on the floor that triggered the silent alarm.

Crow dropped the bags of candy and cartons of milk on the counter, reached into his leather bag, and drew out Jay Anderson's police issue .38 Smith and Wesson. He said, "Put this stuff in a bag and keep your foot off that alarm or I blow a hole in your dumbass face. It just ain't worth it, okay?"

The employee stiffened, his foot still shy two inches from the alarm button. Did he chance it or not?

Not.

Not with the short black barrel of the .38 aimed between his eyes. Instead, he brought out a bag and began to stuff the items into it. His hands were shaking like an old man's. He couldn't stop talking. It was as if a switch had been turned on and he was wound up too tightly to shut up.

"I didn't see that," he said, idiotically. "I didn't see anything. Just take the stuff, mister, and walk out. You want the cash from the register? You can have the cash. Just don't do nothing, okay? Don't do nothing we'll both regret. I've got a kid. My wife left me last month and I'm raising our kid. You don't want to orphan him, do you? You don't want to do anything that would hurt a kid. He's only four, next month, he'll be four, his name's Devon . . ."

It struck Crow as hilarious the stranger was telling him his whole life story. He started to laugh, but a bell sounded as the front door opened and an obese woman strolled straight to the counter. Crow had lowered the gun when he heard the bell. Now the fat woman looked the clerk in the eye and said, "I hope you carry chili powder. I'm not in any mood to drive all the way into town for chili powder. My insurance is high enough, I'm not wanting to run it higher by driving into Fredericksburg and getting in an accident with those fool drivers."

The clerk looked at Crow, then back to the customer. "Uh, I dunno, Bertha . . ."

"I'll look for myself. I don't expect you to come running from behind the counter, I know you have important stuff to do like read the men's magazines you got back there and call your girlfriends on the phone . . ."

"What the hell?" Crow asked, glancing back at the woman making her way down one of the far aisles, still talking.

151

"She's a regular," the clerk said. "She . . . she talks a lot. . . ."

"Someone should put a plug in it."

"Here, just take your stuff, mister." The clerk, his hands still trembling, pushed the bagged goods toward Crow.

The doorbell tinkled again and both of them turned to see a city cop walking in for his daily morning ration of a foot-long hotdog and sixteen-ounce Pepsi. The clerk mumbled, "Oh God."

Crow knew what he had to do and fast. If he hesitated long enough for the cop to realize a man stood in front of the clerk wielding a gun, he'd draw down. Crow swung the revolver at the cop and pulled the trigger three times. Even as the shots rang in Crow's ears, the employee took the opportunity to step on the alarm button before backing away. Crow saw in the man's face what he'd done and shot him point blank in the face, knocking him back against the cold medicine and vitamin display before he fell forward again, dead.

The woman named Bertha came running up the aisle with a spice canister in her fat fist. She was shouting, screaming, coming straight for Crow, as if she would brain him with the plastic spice container.

Death by chili powder, Crow thought crazily. This fat bitch is out of her mind. "Jesus, lady, you're crazy as shit!"

Grabbing the bag of groceries, he leaped over the quickly pooling blood of the cop. He knocked a woman aside who was nearly to the convenience store door to pay for a self-help gas purchase. She screamed and landed on her ass, car keys flying from her hand.

Heddy was out of the van where it was parked in front of the store, motioning with her arms for Crow to hurry. She had seen the cop car drive up and park next to her. She was about to blow the van's horn to get Crow's attention, but she didn't have to. She saw Crow at the counter turn the moment the cop entered.

In the distance sirens screamed, cops making for the convenience store once the silent alarm was logged in at the station.

Crow threw himself into the van and slammed the sliding door. He was white as a drift of new snow except for two high color spots on his cheeks. "Let's get the fuck outta here!"

Bertha burst through the convenience store door, shouting for him to come back, *"Come back right this minute, you crummy little bastard killer!"*

Heddy had the van started and began backing from the parking space when there was a crash that threw them all forwards against the seats. Heddy turned around to try to see out the back tinted windows. Someone opened her door at that exact moment and someone else opened the sliding door at the same time. Crow had put away his gun already so he wasn't prepared for what happened next.

The man who opened Heddy's door hit her in the face with a fist, knocking her over the console and into Jay's lap. He said, "Get outta the way, you stupid bitch."

The man who came from the side of the van pointed a gun at Crow and said, "I'm coming in." He stepped up into the van and pulled the sliding door closed behind him with a bang.

It all happened so swiftly neither Heddy nor Crow had a chance to do anything about it. Heddy, cursing and spitting blood, climbed over the console and into the back. The man there motioned for Carrie and the girl to move back in the van to the next seat, the sofa in the rear. Now he had Heddy and Crow together on one seat. He stood yet, holding himself steady with one hand braced on the ceiling.

"Who are you?" Jay asked, but was ignored.

The man who had hit Heddy and climbed into the driver's seat, put the van into gear. He pulled it forward onto the concrete apron in front of the store, narrowly missing the obese screaming woman who still swung the chili powder in her fist as if it were a live grenade. She scrambled backward on nimble feet and pressed up against the front of the store.

The driver then backed the van out and around the vehicle it had struck before—their car they'd parked in the way to keep their prey from getting away.

He whipped the van from the lot and onto the street, the rear end fishtailing into the opposite lane. He headed the van out of town, north, along the same highway they had just taken into town. At the first farm road, he turned left. At the next farm road, he turned right, and he kept turning left and right on roads until they were in the scrubby hills outside of Fredericksburg and there was no sound of the sirens any longer.

At a sign for a fish camp, the man turned down the road. Dirt blossomed behind the rear of the van, filling the summer noonday air with a dusty cloud that hung motionless.

The camp was closed and up for sale. The man parked the van, screeching to a sliding halt in front of an unpainted cabin that had once served as the office. He turned off the motor.

"We want the money," he said without preamble. "You don't rip off six hundred thousand dollars and think you're gonna keep it."

Heddy looked at Crow, raising one eyebrow. Crow looked up at the man standing over him and said carefully,

"There wasn't no goddamn six hundred grand."

The man winced and glanced at his partner in the driver's seat. "I've got pliers," he said. "Should I use them?"

"I'm telling you, man," Crow said. "There might have been a hundred thousand at most, but nothing at all like six hundred. You got your figures all wrong."

"Okay, Bob," said the driver, nodding at the man in back.

The one called Bob pulled a pair of needle-nosed pliers with plastic-covered handles from his back pocket. "If you don't have the whole six hundred, you're going to lose your nose. You'll never be a pretty boy again."

"I'm telling you . . . !"

Heddy grabbed for her green vinyl bag between the front bucket seats and flung it at the man. "Look for yourself!"

Bob looked at the driver, got another nod, put the pliers back into his pocket. He reached down for the green bag, his gaze still trained on the two in the seat.

"They've got the rest in the extra tire compartment, in the back, outside."

The two men turned to Jay. "Who're you?"

"What does it matter? I know where the money is."

The driver reached out and punched Jay in the face with the same fist he'd used on Heddy. Jay's head hit the closed window and rebounded. He very calmly wiped the trickle of blood running down from his nose over his upper lip. "That wasn't very neighborly."

"Now answer us, smartass. Who're you?"

"I'm Jay Anderson and the woman and little girl in the back are my wife and child. These two took our car in Missouri and we've been with them ever since. Hostages."

The driver looked at Bob. "Check in her purse first."

With his free hand Bob rummaged in the bag and brought out a two-inch packet of bills. He held it up. "This ain't much."

"There's more in Crow's bag," Jay said.

"I ought to . . ." Crow started to say, but the man standing over him slapped his face so hard his head swiveled on his neck.

"Okay, all right. Stop with this heavy goon shit." Crow reached down and brought up his leather satchel to hand over.

The man named Bob rummaged in it and found two more packets of money held together with rubber bands. He shook his head. "It's still not much."

"We're all getting out," said the driver, opening his door. "Now!"

The driver circled the front of the van, waiting while Jay came from the front and Bob and the others stepped down from inside the back of the van. Once Crow, Heddy, and Carrie were out, and the two men waited for the little girl to appear, Jay suddenly took a step back so that he was just to the left and behind the driver. He grabbed him around the neck in a chokehold and threw him forward and down. Heddy dove for the floor of the van and her open purse there while Crow bumped into the other man, knocking him off balance. His gun went off, firing wide. Carrie pulled Emily with her to the ground, covering her head with her own body.

Heddy had her gun. She turned onto her back, brought it up, and fired. The bullet caught Bob just above his ear. It exited the top of his head as a nugget of hot metal, taking with it skull, gristle, and brain that spewed into the sunny air around his head like a bloody halo that dispersed before the body hit the ground.

She then turned the gun on the driver and said to Jay, "Let him go."

The driver stumbled, coughing and choking, holding his throat. He said huskily, "Well, fuck me."

"That's a good idea," Heddy said. "Crow, get your weapon."

Crow stepped over Bob and reached in for his bag. He found the .38 and joined Heddy. He looked down at Carrie and said, "You can get up now."

Carrie stared at her husband with stunned eyes. "What have you done?" she asked.

Jay looked only mildly surprised at his own actions. He frowned, thinking, and then he smiled. "I think I just saved our lives."

"They'll keep coming after you," the driver said to Heddy and Crow. "You don't walk off with Esponza's loot and think you'll get away with it."

"Esponza's a fucking Spic shithead," Crow said.

"He thinks the same of you, Walker."

Heddy grimaced at the usage of Crow's real name. "What's this about six hundred grand?"

"It's what you took. It's what we had in the house, on the tables. Six hundred and change, actually. If you don't give it back . . ."

Heddy looked at Crow. Crow had taken the money from the tables while she had the men in the house lie down on the floor, hands taped and resting above their heads. She had been busy, much too busy to watch him round up the cash. Crow took the money, Crow knew about the money. What a lousy thing to do to her. What a really crummy lowlife kind of deal that was. Here they'd been on the road for days now since the heist and he hadn't said a word to her.

Crow glanced over at her and said, "Don't fucking look at me, I don't have it."

"We don't have it," she said, sounding righteous. "You can count what we got and then you go back and tell them. You tell them someone else took the rest, it wasn't us."

"They're not going to believe that."

"It was on the tables?"

"Yeah."

"It was stacked up and rubber-banded and it was all right there in the open. On the tables? When we hit the house?"

"That's what I said."

"You've been misinformed. It's a fucking lie," Heddy said, her voice rising in anger.

The driver shook his head slowly. "I think your boy-friend's holding out."

Heddy looked at Crow again. "You holding out? Huh, Crow? Is he fucking lying or did you make off with more than I thought?"

"I told you, no! Shit, look in my bag. You saw what he pulled out. Where you think I hid it, up my goddamn ass?"

Heddy knew he was lying, she knew Crow, and he was fucking lying. The thought caught her way down in her gut and made it burn, like pouring rubbing alcohol over an open sore. Yet she said again to the driver, "Tell them we don't have it, we didn't take it. A hundred grand's not gonna break nobody. Tell them to leave us the fuck alone or we'll kill every fucking bonehead comes after us. You tell them that."

Heddy waved Jay, Carrie, and the girl back into the van. Crow patted the driver down and found no weapon. "You stupid goon," Crow said.

They left him standing next to the body of his dead partner as they drove away from the deserted fish camp.

Heddy was driving, as usual, with Jay in the seat next to her. "You saved our asses," she said. "I'm not much for saying thanks, but that was really something."

"Then you can do something for me."

"I'm not letting you go."

"Then let Carrie and Em go. I earned their freedom. Take me with you."

Heddy glanced over her shoulder at Crow. He shook his head.

She said, "I can't do that. Crow's attached to them. You'll have to talk to Crow."

"Wait till we get to the border," Crow said. "I'd feel better if we wait."

Jay cleared his throat. "You sure Crow didn't take the rest of that money?"

"I think you better butt out," Crow said, danger creeping into his tone.

"If he did, I'll find it," Heddy said, not willing to talk about the betrayal with Jay. She could not deal with it right now. It made her stomach hurt. She grimaced as she clutched the wheel, driving as fast as she dared away from the fish camp. She turned onto a highway leading away from the town of Fredericksburg. She'd had quite enough of the place before she ever hit the city limits.

"We have to get another car," she said.

"I was afraid of that." Crow found the bag of goodies from the convenience store pushed under the seat and brought out an Almond Joy bar. He handed it to Carrie and smiled at her.

The little girl looked at him as if he had snakes crawling on his head. "Don't worry, I'll give you something," he said, but he didn't think that was the problem. He didn't think that was what was in her thoughts at all.

* * * * *

The minute I knew Crow had double-crossed Heddy, I wondered how long it would be before she killed him.

The men after us wanted back six hundred thousand dollars. I tried to think how much that is, but I couldn't do it. I've never had more than a ten-dollar allowance to spend by myself. I tried to imagine thousands of ten-dollar bills piled up and I just couldn't work it out in my head how many piles it would take, how many tens would have to be in each pile. Mama always told me I needed to study harder in math.

When Heddy asked Crow about the money, he made a joke of it and said where would he have it hidden anyway?

Then I saw behind his eyes and inside his head and I knew where he had it hidden. I knew everything. It was like seeing a movie at fast speed, or fast-forwarding a VCR tape. I wasn't in the van anymore. My own thoughts were re-placed. I went spinning into the memories that Crow had opened up with what had just happened to us and how he was being accused and had to save his face. I stopped being me. I became Craig Walker.

I was at a door to a house, a back door, the day was cloudy and there had just been rain. I could smell the grass, crushed down by their feet as they padded across it to the gray cinder path leading up to the door. I was seeing all this as if through Crow's eyes.

Heddy knocked and called out, telling them she was there to see her friend, Rory. "Hey, Rory," she yelled and knocked some more. "It's me, Heddy."

"He's not here, go away," someone called through the door.

Heddy grinned her crooked half grin at Crow hiding beside the steps, gun drawn, and banged on the door again, not to be denied. "He said I could wait for him here. Hey, man, how about if I pick up some rocks while I'm here anyway, 'kay?"

Sounds of bolts being thrown and chains coming unchained rattled through the quiet morning. The door opened and a Mexican man who could have stood to lose some weight around his middle hovered there frowning at her. He said, "Who the fuck are you, man?"

Crow came from his crouch beside the steps, out of sight, and moved up the steps where Heddy had stepped aside. "No, the question is, man, who the fuck are *you?*"

He pushed the guy back and moved into what used to be a big open kitchen. It was still a kitchen, but on the counters there were lab supplies, beakers, tubes, vials. And something cooking, dripping from a rubber tube into a huge glass jar. There were trays of junk, trays of rock, trays of powder, a whole arsenal of pharmaceutical shock-joy-toys.

Two guys sat at a huge makeshift table made with wide smooth planks laid across sawhorses. They were counting money, putting rubber bands on it, stacking it to the side. Now they stopped, hands frozen in place. Another man came from the front of the house and stopped in the doorway to the kitchen. He said, "Whoa . . ." He was so big, he filled the doorway, but the blood drained from his face instantly when he saw it was a heist.

"Everyone get up slow-like and move out," Crow said, twitching the gun at the seated men at the money table.

They rose and, with the man who had opened the door, joined the fourth man in the doorway. They all trooped into the next room that had once been a family living room. Now there was just a broken spring sofa, torn and leaking gray cotton, sitting beneath a window where the blinds were shut. Gloom camped in the corners of the room and dust motes danced lazily through the spear of sunshine leaking through the small square window in the front door. Empty pizza boxes and Chinese take-out cartons, overflowing ashtrays and empty beer cans littered the floor.

On the sofa sat two guys playing poker on the sofa cushion between them. They looked up, startled, and dropped their cards. Some of them fluttered to the floor.

"Get them down," Crow said to Heddy.

She brought out her own gun she'd bought off Bandy and told them to get on the floor on their bellies. "Don't fucking stand there, do it! I look like Mary Poppins to you?"

Crow backed into the kitchen, his gaze shifting from man to man as they obeyed Heddy. He took a black Hefty leaf bag from his pocket. He flapped it open and began pushing the money packets into it. He could feel his heart stampeding like a herd of buffalo and his mouth went bone dry. He swallowed hard, but he couldn't stop grinning, thinking how much money this was, how *fucking much money he had his hands on.*

When it was all inside, he tied the top and dropped it

to the floor for pick up on their way out. He moved into the living room again. He saw Heddy had done a fine job, a really highly excellent round up, top caliber. The six men were all on the floor, lined up like bodies in a morgue, hands above their heads. She'd taped their wrists with gray duct tape, tearing each piece with her teeth.

Crow didn't hesitate, didn't have time. Someone else might come in any minute or some drug-crazed fiend might knock at the door, wanting to buy some shit.

Stepping to the first man in the line, Crow leaned down and put a bullet into his skull. Moving fast, not thinking, going blank as a slate chalkboard, he did the same to the next and the next. The fourth man had rolled over by then and put up his hands in some kind of plea. Crow plugged him in the forehead and heard the eerie shattering laughter coming from Heddy that did a tornado spin up the column of his spine. He shivered and moved on. They were crazy, he and Heddy, he knew that, but this was the craziest thing he'd ever pulled in his life. Wholesale slaughter wasn't just a picnic in the park. It was doing stuff to his mind and freaking him out completely.

The fifth man was on his knees, trying to crawl backward like a crawfish, but Crow stopped him easy. The last man made it to the door before Crow dropped him with two shots to the back. Heddy went to him and shot him again, in the head.

It was all over in minutes, less than ten minutes and they were rich, so filthy stinking fucking almighty rich they'd never work again, never lift a finger to earn their bread. It was crazy, it was horrible, it was totally unjustified, but it was also so exhilarating that Crow wanted to climb the walls, eat glass, and fuck horses.

That night he and Heddy stayed at a dump with torn linoleum floors and a bed that sagged in the center. They were on the edge of St. Louis, somewhere where white people wouldn't even drive at night, much less take a room. A great place to hide.

She wanted to see the money, sort it, count it, but he told her the truth. He had to get balled or he was going to blow a nut. They screwed their brains out and fell asleep a little after midnight.

The next morning, Crow woke at six a.m. It was prison life made him crack open his eyes and look around suspiciously. Prison made him get his ass moving not long after dawn and he hadn't shaken the habit yet. His body clock was still striking morning wake-up call no matter how late he'd been up the night before.

Heddy had drunk about a quart of Mr. Jim and she was out, cold as a tombstone. Crow knew she would be, counted on it. He quietly rose from bed, dressed, and stuffed the majority of the money from the heavy Hefty bag into his leather satchel. Then he let himself out the motel door while Heddy snored in a blubbery drunken sleep that left spit bubbles forming between her open lips.

He drove to an office supply store and bought a large manila mailer full of bubble plastic. In the car again he took the money from his satchel and got most of it into the mailer. He sealed the envelope and addressed it to himself at:

CRAIG WALKER
DUPRAVADO HOTEL
BROWNSVILLE, TEXAS

Heddy didn't know he'd already made reservations for them and that he'd told the manager he would be expecting a package they could hold for him until he got there.

Heddy would never know about the money.

It's not that he didn't love Heddy, hell, he loved her enough—or he thought he did and wasn't that the same thing? Squirreling away the money was just what you did when you had made a promise to yourself that you'd never again in this lifetime spend years behind bars in a goddamn maximum security prison. It's just what you did when all your life the people you trusted fucked you over. You didn't look out for Number One, no one did, even Heddy could understand that.

No matter how long Heddy was his old lady, there was no way in hell she'd ever know he had the haul stashed away for when they might need it.

He bought a book of stamps at a convenience store, stamped the package with every stamp, and dropped it in a blue mailbox on the street before picking up coffee and Egg McMuffins to take back to Heddy.

Then Mama shook me and she was calling my name, repeating it. "Emily. Emily! What's wrong? Emily!"

When I blinked, the van was back and I was back. I didn't want to look at Crow because if I looked at him, he'd know I knew, he'd understand some way that I knew where the money was and how he'd cheated and lied to Heddy.

"Mama? I'm okay. I'm okay."

"She have a seizure or what? What the hell's wrong with her? I never seen a kid act like that." Crow sounded wound tight.

165

Heddy said from the driver's seat, "If she throws up, I'll dump her out on the road."

Mama hugged me close to her bosom and I wanted to cry, but that would just make things worse.

"What happened to you?" she asked.

Daddy was concerned too. He was twisted around in the seat, looking worried.

"I don't know, Mama, I . . ."

"You wouldn't speak to me. You just sat there with your head all loose and rolling around, but your eyes were open. Are you sure you're all right?"

"See what you're doing to my family?" Daddy asked. "She probably needs a doctor. You're scaring her to death."

"I'm . . . I'm all right. I'm really all right."

She's probably hysterical because her father betrayed us, Mama thought.

I didn't want to hear anyone's thoughts anymore. I pulled away from my mother and sat up straight. I breathed real deep and then held my breath for a couple of seconds. I thought about school and doing my lessons. I thought about history and the Battle of Shiloh, something we had been studying at the end of the school year. I thought about computers and wondered if I'd ever get one like some of the kids in my class had in their rooms at home. I thought about the blanket I had when I was little, how soft and yellow it was, covered all over with little white ducks, how I hugged it against me in bed at night and felt safe and warm.

For the next hour all I thought about was me and stuff about my life and memories of my past. That squeezed out Crow and Mama so that I wasn't a tuning fork picking up their stray thoughts.

But I couldn't help wondering if we'd be with Crow and Heddy when they got to Brownsville. If they ever got to

Brownsville so they could cross over to Matamoras. And what would happen when Heddy found out a big, thick, manila package packed with money was waiting there at the check-in for her boyfriend.

* * * * *

That night everyone was subdued and silent, even Crow, who didn't touch his bag to hunt down a high. Heddy watched him tie the family and pull the covers over them as if tucking in his own children.

When Crow was in the shower, Heddy sat down on the bed next to Jay and said quietly, "You really did save us back at that fish camp. If it hadn't been for you, I don't think we would have walked away alive."

Jay turned on his side toward her and away from his wife, who lay on her side facing the other direction. He smiled a little at Heddy.

Heddy let her hand rest on his shoulder. She dragged it down his arm, squeezed his elbow, and then slid her hand down over his chest. She felt his intake of breath and how he stiffened.

"I think I really do like you," she said. Carrie began to turn onto her back. "You stay where you are. I'm not talking to you." Carrie halted and she too got stiff.

Heddy glanced at the closed bathroom door, heard the shower running. She then leaned down to Jay and kissed him full on the lips. When she moved back a little, she saw his eyes open on her. She saw in those eyes what she wanted to see.

"We need to talk," she said. "Later."

She stood from the bed and left him there, slightly bewildered and, she hoped, excited by what she'd done. All night she thought of him, even in her dreams. She'd wake from them, breathing heavy and feeling like touching herself. She'd fall asleep again, thinking of him in the other bed, so close yet so far.

Surely Crow could see she was getting stuck on the guy. They didn't have to talk about this. It was just something that happened. Just because Jay was a cop didn't mean she couldn't get hot for him.

And anyway, he'd saved their lives. He wasn't much of a cop, not much of one at all.

She thought he wanted her too. She would bet all the money Crow said they didn't have on it.

★ ★ ★ ★ ★

The next day on the road, not far from Choke Canyon Lake, outside of Tilden, Texas on Route 16, the van began to sway from a low rear tire.

Heddy stood sweating over Jay as he changed it. She told the woman and kid to stay inside the vehicle, give her no trouble. Crow wandered off from the road, peering across the empty, low hilly landscape with a hand up to his eyes to block the sun.

"You want to go to Mexico with me?" Heddy asked Jay in a low voice so Crow couldn't hear. She'd been thinking about it all night. This was the right thing to do. This was what she wanted almost more than she wanted the money. The only lovers she'd ever been with were cons, ex-cons, losers, and junkies. She'd never had a straight-up boyfriend, a guy who didn't mangle the language, didn't speak street lingo, didn't want to jump her in broad daylight in the back of a hot car or up against the wall in some alleyway. It was time to try someone new, someone from across the tracks in the nice, clean middleclass world.

He looked up at her, squinting against the sunlight. He had great eyes, she thought. Dark brown, deep, strong and sure of what they wanted out of life. His shirt was off and his back was going from soft pink to blistering red even as she watched. He had good shoulders, if too white and tender. They were square and muscled. He was in good shape, a much better specimen of man than Crow could ever hope to be. She caught herself dreaming—even as she stood staring at his shoulders—about the night she got him hard and rode him right into heaven. She wanted that again. Over and over, every day, every night. She couldn't remember ever wanting somebody that bad. Certainly not Crow.

"Is that an offer?" He glanced over at where Crow had moved further into the barrenness that bracketed the farm highway.

"It depends on how much you like being a cop."

"I never liked it. I never fucking liked it."

She smiled her half smile then put her hand over her mouth to conceal it. "I thought as much. Big as you are, good as you move, there were a couple of times you could have taken Crow out and you didn't. There's something on your mind."

He turned back to the chore of screwing off lug nuts from the wheel. "You might be right."

169

"You wouldn't miss your wife and kid?"

"I'd . . ." he paused turning a lug nut and wiped sweat from his brow. "I'd miss Emily."

"Even though you'd miss her, you could leave?"

"I think so. It would probably be better for her if I weren't around anyway."

"Think you could help us disappear once we get across the border? Help with new identities, stuff like that?"

"I could probably do that. I know some tricks." Again he glanced at Crow, wandering away from the road. "What about him?"

Heddy made a little dismissive sound in the back of her throat. "He doesn't like you, but he does what I say."

"Are you sure about that? Even when it comes to me? I never heard of a threesome that lasted."

"I'm sure. It'll last as long as I want it to."

"I've got to tell you something . . ."

"Yeah?"

"He took the money."

Heddy frowned hard at Crow's receding back. "I know," she said. "I've already figured that out."

"You know what he did with it?"

"Not yet. I'll find out."

"You'll need it. Living's not free, even south of the border. Especially when you don't want to be noticed."

"We'll all need it. Don't worry, let me handle Crow."

Jay finished taking off the last lug nut and worked the flat tire off. He stood up, leaning the tire against the van's fender. "You don't hurt Carrie or Em. You don't do that. If you do that, I'll do whatever I have to do to take *both* of you out. I promise it."

Heddy looked into his eyes. A flirty smile slipped across her lips and away again. "I'll let them go."

170

"You better mean it."

Heddy pushed out her breasts, arching her back. "I hate useless women, but I'll let 'em go. In return, you help me make Crow hand over the rest of the stash."

Now he grinned, sweat trickling into his eyes, stinging them, making him squint like a Clint Eastwood character. "I can do that," he said and turned to put on the spare. "To tell you the truth, I'd like nothing better."

*   *   *   *   *

How was I going to tell my mother? Heddy made us stay in the stifling hot van while Daddy changed the tire, but Heddy didn't know I could peek in on her thoughts anytime I wanted to. I peeked and my heart felt like a rubber ball someone was squeezing. I gasped. Mama took hold of both my hands and said, "What's wrong, Em? Are you sick again?"

How was I going to tell her? I couldn't do it. She had wanted to leave him, but for him to leave her—this way— was something I couldn't tell her about.

I tried to imagine what life would be without Daddy— totally without him, as if he had died. If we'd left him in North Carolina, at least I would have seen him once in a while. Mama would have worked out visiting arrangements. It wouldn't have been like he stopped being my Daddy.

But this way, with him willing to change his whole life, giving up the law to go off with Heddy—well, I'd never see him again. Ever. I knew that. One day Heddy would probably kill him. One day when she was tired of him or mad. Or one day Crow would do it, behind Heddy's back, and he'd call it an accident. Or the Mexican police would find them and put them all in a dark prison for the rest of their lives.

It made me so sad that I wanted to crawl under some covers on a bed and never come out. I knew now what Mama felt like when she'd been hit for doing nothing wrong. I just wanted to be very quiet, not move, not do anything, not eat, not talk, and not know what people thought. I wanted to be still like a fish that lives in black caves deep in the sea, never seeing the sunlight at all.

I put my head down on the seat and told Mama I was tired. I shut my eyes and tried to dream. If I could just dream, I wouldn't know anything about all this. I wouldn't know about all the killing and all the dead people. Or about Daddy and how he'd changed, how he'd let the bad moon loony come into his head and stay there, spreading evil.

I might have been ready for it if I'd ever tried to listen to Daddy's thoughts. But I'd been too busy linking up, against my will most times, with Crow and Heddy. I thought I knew what my Daddy believed and what he would do if given the chance. He was a policeman! Even when he'd helped Heddy and Crow with the two killers sent to collect the money, it didn't occur to me that it meant what it really meant. That he wanted to be an outlaw—he was saving the outlaws so he could be one too. The only way to be an outlaw, the only opportunity he'd ever been granted was on this trip with two deadly stone-crazy murderers.

He wanted to be like them. He wanted to hide out in Mexico. He wanted Heddy more than he wanted us.

As if we'd never existed.

It was like he'd died on me. The Daddy I had known, as

bad as he sometimes was to my mother, had died somewhere between Missouri and Texas. It was just his body
that kept going. Now Mama and I were really on our own.
It made me feel so lonely that I wanted to die.

* * * * *

Crow walked away from the van while Jay changed the flat
tire. At least their hostage was good for something, he re-
flected. Hell, if *he* wanted to change goddamn tires in the
middle of the day with the sun like a furnace. He did not,
no sir, like scut work.

Hugging the road was a shallow, dry, pebble-lined ditch.
He crossed it and walked into the desert land that rolled
into the distance with small hills dotted with scrub brush.
There wasn't a fence here the way there usually was on land
running beside a highway. But then who would want to own
this desert? What was it good for? Overhead the sun burned
with blinding white light so that the horizon in the great far
distance was hazy, a gray icing on the lip of the world. Between the horizon and where Crow walked shimmered heat
mirages that danced no more than a foot above the beige
cracked ground.

Crow stopped. He took a deep breath of hot air. He
had never been in the Southwest before, never walked
onto such a large section of dry land, never imagined how
far he could see, as if to the rim of eternity. The sky was
so wide and pale that it was oppressive. With only a little
imagination he could feel himself tentatively anchored to

the planet while it twirled crazily in space.

He had been told by a guy in prison, Prentice, that the Earth revolved at a thousand miles an hour and it was only gravity and God's grace that kept man from being flung off into the void. Prentice read science magazines and tattered copies of science fiction novels. He was a pretty smart guy.

Crow hadn't paid much attention to Prentice then, nodding and playing a game of checkers with him very competitively, hated to lose. But now he could feel it, what Prentice said. Out here in the Texas heat, overcome by the wide expanse of sky, the horizon standing open and empty, he knew just how insignificant he was and how fragile his existence.

He spit on the ground and frowned. Best not to think about it, about motion, about moving through space even when he couldn't feel it. It made him too jittery. The hit of speed didn't help, of course. He shouldn't have done so much of it. He'd hoped getting away from the van and the others would calm his nerves. The muscles in his jaw jumped like gear wheels with missing teeth.

He squatted and picked up a handful of sand and rock to jiggle up and down in his palm. Would Mexico be this hot, this desolate? Goddamn, he'd hate it. He let the gritty sand drift through splayed fingers. How any of the scrubby, ground-hugging trees lived in this soil just amazed him.

He glanced over his shoulder to check Jay's progress with the tire. He saw him standing, talking with Heddy. Something wasn't quite right with the scene. Usually Heddy was exasperated with their hostages, especially Jay. About the only thing she ever said to him was to shut up. Yet now they stood like two old friends in the exercise yard at Leavenworth, shooting the shit.

Crow squinted and from holding so still felt the sun

scorching his back through the material of his shirt. He turned back and stared at the sand between his knees. Heddy and Jay. Talking. Big buddies. Taking time in this fearsome heat with the sun squeezing the moisture out of their pores, talking while he was away from them. Secret talk. And about what, he wondered? What if they were discussing the missing money?

That's what they were talking about!

He stood abruptly and moved toward the road and the van. What did this mean for him if Heddy had a thing for Jay and she didn't trust him anymore? If she thought they were going to share the loot with him, she had another think coming. He wouldn't even share it with *her* if she decided to bring Jay in on the deal.

On top of which, he absolutely loathed the man. He silently wished they had never run into the family at the caverns. He wished they had never taken their car and then brought them along for protection and security. Not this far. Too far! First it had been at Heddy's insistence and now it was at his. They'd both made a big mistake.

The whole trip had been muddled up because the Andersons were along. He and Heddy had to watch them, feed them, tie them up, take them to the bathroom. They'd turned into babysitters. He didn't care that Jay had saved their asses at the fishing camp. Hell, he would have thought of something. Or Heddy would have. He didn't have to be beholden to a cop, for fuck's sake.

As Crow neared the van, Jay was just letting down the jack and beginning to put away the tools. Heddy had already moved around the van to the driver's door. Crow said to Jay's sweaty back, "She's some piece of work, huh?"

Jay flinched, not having heard Crow's approach from the

ditch. He held still before saying, "You're howling up the wrong tree, Monkey Man."

It wasn't the name he'd been called that caused Crow to respond so instantly and violently. It was Jay's tone of voice, a mocking, go-to-hell tone. Before he knew he'd done it, Crow sucker-punched the other man in the kidneys. It was enough of a shot to take him to his knees. He didn't stay down, though, and Crow wasn't ready for the complete explosion of fury that whirled up from the ground into his face. Jay got him in the left eye, knocking him flat on his butt, scraping the palms of his hands in gravel as he caught himself.

Crow howled. Lights bloomed in his field of vision before receding to allow him to see Jay standing nearby, fists clenched. Crow scrabbled to his knees, to his feet, and went in toward Jay's stomach with his head low. He'd really hurt the motherfucker now. He'd kill him! This was his chance to make everything right again.

Jay stepped aside at the last moment and this caused Crow to barrel headlong into the rear of the van. It knocked him back a step and brought back the burst of lights.

Someone had him by the arm. He twisted to lob a swing and checked it by one second when he saw it was Heddy who had hold of him. She was screaming something at him, but his head still rang from the fist in the eye and the thud his head took from the van.

He shook himself, glared at Jay. "I hate this son of a bitch."

He could hear Heddy now. "You stop it, stop it right now, Crow. We've got to get on the road. I won't have this fighting, do you hear me? You're slowing us down, you're just fucking up, Crow, that's all you're doing."

"I hear you, but I don't fucking believe you. Why are

176

you taking up for this bastard?"

Heddy's gaze flicked away from him to Jay. He read it all in that one action. She was moving away from him, her emotions were swaying toward the other man; she was being won away. What a goddamn luckless thing to happen.

"He'll fuck you over, Heddy. Don't you know that?"

"Why don't you let me worry about it? Last time I looked, you didn't own me. Now get in the damn van."

He watched her stalk off, gave Jay one last scowl, and left him standing at the back of the van. Inside, sitting next to the little girl, he shook with anger. His eye was already swelling shut and it hurt, it hurt like holy hell. He could hardly see out of it for the tearing. "Whatta you looking at?" he said to the kid. "Look somewhere else." He ran a hand over the sparse hair on his shaved scalp.

Emily scooted away from him on the bench seat. The front passenger door opened and Jay slipped inside.

"Next time, I kill you," Crow said to him softly.

"Not if I kill you first."

Heddy started the van and pulled onto the road. "Shut up," she said. "Both of you shut the fuck up."

* * * * *

It was after midnight before Heddy had driven them south across the state to the border at Brownsville, Texas. They had tried to find another vehicle to switch to, but nothing looked available. Heddy stopped twice for gas and to let everyone use the bathrooms. She wouldn't stop for food, making them eat service station fare consisting of chips and stale packaged cookies.

By the time they rolled into Brownsville, Crow was wide awake, his insides jangling from not getting a regular hit of speed. He twitched where he sat on the edge of the seat, watching the signs taking them into the town. "Let's stay in a hotel and cross over tomorrow," he said.

"Sounds okay to me," Heddy said. "My legs are cramped and I feel like I've driven around the world."

It was simple to get Heddy to turn in the parking area for the Dupravado Hotel. The building stood in the center of the sleeping downtown along the main drag. It was an older, three-story structure made of earthy brown brick. A neon sign hung before the entrance, half the letters burned out. It wasn't exactly a high class joint, being way too far down into the old downtown section, but it was within walking distance to the border crossing and that's what mattered. One of the Mexican inmates in Leavenworth had told him about it. "I come from dere, man," he said proudly, meaning Brownsville. "The Dupravado, she right smack in de center of town and close to the border."

Before Heddy hardly had the van in a parking slot nosed in next to the building, Crow was out the sliding side door. "I'll go sign us in and try to get two connecting rooms if they have them."

He sprinted across the white gravel lot toward the entrance. His moon shadow flitted before him like a nervous ghost. He had to make it inside before Heddy could see him pick up the package waiting at the desk. That meant hurrying, hurrying, practically jogging.

The hotel clerk was Hispanic, very dark, almost black.

He seemed to understand Crow's urgency—just as if he'd seen this furtive anxiety before. One eyebrow rose in query when he handed over the package that had come in the mail last week. Crow thanked him and hit him with a ten spot. The clerk smiled and stuffed the bill into his pocket. Money made everything smooth, Crow noted; it made the world his fat oyster.

While Crow forced the manila package into his large leather satchel, eyeing the door all the while, the clerk began to fill out the register in the name of Craig Walker. Crow grabbed the register suddenly and said, "Let me change this." He took the pen from the clerk and changed the name to read: Howard Bradley. When he turned the pad back around for the clerk, he smiled widely.

The clerk just glanced at the name and said nothing. Crow waited and finally it came clear to him. The clerk was waiting for more dough. Changing a name in the register cost.

Crow hauled another ten from his pocket and handed it over. "There. Think that'll cover it?"

The clerk smiled, revealing crooked bottom teeth, and closed the registry. He did not ask for identification. This was Brownsville where illegals crossed over the Rio Grande river from Mexico. They came in the dead of night to head for the interior of Texas. Whether the guest was Hispanic or white, there wasn't any point in taking down IDs, most of which would have proven false if checked out. Management didn't care about much but the nightly fees.

The clerk took the money from Crow for two connecting rooms before glancing at the door to see a man, two women, and a child enter the front door. "Your party?" he asked, amused. Crow wondered what he'd been expecting, a few grungy gangster types?

179

"Yeah, that's them. You got the keys?"

The clerk handed over the keys and said, "You look familiar. Ever been on TV?"

Crow gave him a fishy eye. "How 'bout I talk to you about that later?" It was a promise that, given time and privacy, the clerk would get more than the twenty bucks. Only if he kept his mouth closed, of course.

Crow joined the others and led them to the elevator at the end of the lobby. He hoped Heddy wouldn't notice the extra bulge in his bag. The only way she'd get hold of the money was to kill him first. And that prick, Jay, would certainly never get it.

He almost stopped in his tracks, so taken aback was he by the random thought. Was that what she was up to with Jay? Using Jay to dispose of him so they could share the stash? He *hated* thinking paranoid thoughts like that. Heddy was his partner. Without her he wouldn't even be here. He wished he could trust her again, *goddamn it,* he wished things were clearer to him.

When Heddy asked him in the elevator what floor button to push, he snarled at her, "Two."

"What're you biting my head off for?"

She was tired from driving and in no mood for his antics, he knew that. He tried to smooth it over. "I need some sleep."

"Well, you're not the only one, stop being such a jerk." She added, "You get two rooms?"

"Yeah. We'll have some privacy for a goddamn change."

The elevator door opened and Crow went out first to lead them to the room numbers. He kept the leather satchel in front of his body, out of their line of vision. Nobody was taking his money from him. Nogoddamnbody.

Frank teamed up with the FBI's ongoing investigation in St. Louis. It was discovered that on Prairie Avenue only days before there had been a report from neighbors of gun shots. When police checked it out, they naturally went to the known drug house they hadn't yet been able to shut down. There, with a search warrant, they found blood on the floor of the living area; enough bloodstains to indicate massive murders had taken place. But the house was empty, totally deserted now. The drug operation had moved on. And whatever bodies had lain in that blood had also been moved.

"Rory" was one Rory Rodriguez, minor drug felon, two-time loser. He had been found dead at a service station out of state. An employee at the station remembered a pearl white Riviera that left not long before the body was discovered.

They were headed south.

Frank, along with FBI agents in conference, tried to figure out the connection between Craig Walker, Rory Rodriguez, and the evidence of blood left in the drug house on Prairie Avenue. It didn't take much to postulate there might have been robbery involved. They'd stolen money for their flight from the Mexican gangs.

And they were still headed south, considering where Rory had been found. But the route appeared to be a strange one, leading across the state of Missouri into Kansas and only then turning south.

The bodies of the Anderson family had not yet been found. Frank and the agents all believed now the family was still with Craig and the girlfriend. It was a cross-country push with three hostages in tow.

Frank had to give the FBI what he knew about Jay Anderson. They weren't too impressed with Jay's background and credentials. He was in therapy? He beat his wife? What a scum.

Frank didn't tell them he feared Jay might crack and do anything. Even join in on the spree, a lawman gone bad to the bone. And if the young criminal couple had Jay helping them out, they might actually skip the country alive. It sure increased their chances.

* * * * *

Crow put us all in one bed together—Mama, Daddy, and me. Afterward I heard him and Heddy taking a shower in the other room, making lots of noise, and laughing. They were near to the border and escape. The thought must have made them happy.

I couldn't move around much because my ankles were tied and I didn't have much room between my parents. After a little while I got so hot, I was sweating. I whispered, "Mama, could you move over a little bit? I'm hot."

She didn't say anything so I tapped her on the shoulder. She was turned on her side away from me. Daddy lay on his back, both his hands and feet tied and looped together down the front of him.

Mama still didn't say anything or move over.

Daddy said, "She's asleep, Em. She's tired out." He scooted over a little to give me more room.

"Daddy?"

"Yes?"

"Are you really going to Mexico tomorrow with Heddy?"

He was quiet for a little while. "How do you know about that?"

"I don't see how you can do it."

"Emily, I asked you how you knew about it."

I squirmed, trying to find a cool spot on the sheets. "I heard you and Heddy talking."

"You were in the van."

"I still heard."

"Does your mother know?"

"No, she didn't hear."

We were whispering, but Daddy raised his head off the pillow to see if Mama was awake and listening now. He dropped his head back down, sighing.

"You don't understand," he said. "I wish I could explain it, but I don't think I can."

"I'll never see you again if you go."

"Sure you will! I'll send for you to visit sometimes." He hesitated. "I guess that's not true. I won't be able to do that. Not until you're older, a lot older.

"Your mother was going to take you away from me anyway, Em. We were separating when we got back home. This is no different."

If he thought this was the same thing, I didn't know what to think. "I'll never see you again," I repeated. I had to tell him the truth. "Why do you . . . like . . . her?" He knew I meant Heddy.

"It's complicated. Maybe I don't know exactly all the

183

reasons why myself. She's . . . she's not like other women."

"She's not like Mama, that's for sure. Daddy, she's killed people. She should go to jail. If you're with her, you'll go to jail too."

He was quiet again for a while. "If we're caught, yeah, I guess I will."

"And Crow doesn't like you."

"I don't like him either."

"He hid that money from Heddy."

"I know he did. He's a real jerk. A stupid punk kid." Daddy lifted his head again to see if he could see past the door that connected the two rooms. Like me, he could hear the two of them in the shower, playing around.

"What if Crow gets really mad about you and Heddy? When you get down to Mexico? What if he . . . ?"

"Emily, you're just going to have to stop worrying about me. I'm a grown man. I can take care of myself. And your mother will make sure to take good care of you. You'll be better off without me around."

He was right, Mama and I would both be better off, but he was still my father. I couldn't believe what he was going to do. I had to try to stop him. "You're a policeman, Daddy. You're supposed to arrest people like them."

"Sometimes, Em, people change."

I didn't know if he meant Crow and Heddy might change or that he had. I said, "Sheriff Eric won't know what to think."

Daddy let out a small grunt. "He'll think he'll have to hire a new recruit, that's all. He never liked me all that much. He's the one who sent me down to Charlotte to talk to . . ."

"Who?"

"Never mind."

It seemed I couldn't find a way to persuade my father not to carry out his plan to leave the country. All I could think to say, at last, was, "She's dangerous."

"I know. Don't worry. Try not to worry. I really do love you, Em. I always have. I can't help how I am. Things haven't been right for me and your mother for a long time."

We both heard the door to the hall open and lifted our heads from the bed to see who had come in. We saw the hotel clerk cross our doorway, glance in, then turn for the bathroom where Crow and Heddy showered.

"What's he want?" I asked Daddy.

"I don't know, baby. But I think you ought to wake up your mother. Something's going on."

$$* \quad * \quad * \quad * \quad *$$

Heddy wasn't as tired as she had pretended. Once Crow had the family bound and in the bed in the other room, Heddy pounced on him as he undressed for the shower. She came from behind snaking one hand between his legs to cup his balls and one hand around the front of him, taking his penis into her hand.

"I'm horny as hell," she whispered against his neck, then licked where her breath had laid down a track of moist heat.

"Let me get a shower. Join me?"

She let him go and began ripping off her clothes as if they were on fire.

"I thought you were tired."

"Not when I walk in the bathroom and catch you naked,

185

those tight little buns staring me down. God, I love your butt."

"You kinky bitch. C'mere." He drew her into his arms and ran his tongue around her lips, then into her mouth.

They played like children in the shower, soaping one another down, playing slapstick games, slipping, sliding, colliding—and laughing all the while with uproarious squeals and squawks.

He tried to push inside her while she braced herself with her feet against the tub rim, back against the wall, but they both slipped, nearly ripping down the shower curtain. He gave it up as a bad job until Heddy went down on her knees and took him in her mouth. He wrapped his hands in the wet tangles of her hair and groaned in pleasure as the shower beat down on his shoulders. "Oh Heddy, oh baby . . ."

Neither of them heard the door to the room open and someone pad across the thin carpet to the partially open bathroom door. It wasn't until the man there spoke that they halted their shenanigans, Heddy rising to her feet. Crow slipped aside the shower curtain, his erection immediately shrinking.

"You can go down the hall to the fire exit, up the fire escape to the roof, cross over, and down the escape on the other side."

It was the chocolate-dark Hispanic clerk who had signed them in. Crow gaped at him. "What the fuck you talking about, man? What the FUCK are you doing in here?"

"I sent two bad dudes on a wild goose. They right now knocking on the door of an empty room on the first floor looking for you. Me, I'm going down the service elevator and out the back before they come up here. I think you better move it. After you pay me first."

Heddy ripped aside the curtain, standing boldly in her

nakedness, water from the showerhead sluicing down her thin body. The clerk never blinked an eyelash. She said, "They asked for us?"

"They asked for a guy named Crow, but when they described him, I knew it was you." He pointed at Crow, then smiled grimly. "They didn't even bother to hide the guns they were carrying. They're bad dudes. Real forward."

Crow viciously turned the water faucet handles and stepped out. He was covered with goosebumps and not from the chill of the air. His penis had further shriveled into near nonexistence, hiding on top of his tight balls like a sparrow ducking in a birdhouse from the onslaught of a hawk.

Wrapping a towel around his middle, he hurried into the bedroom and found a packet of the money for the clerk. "Here, take this."

"Wow, all right, that's cool, *gracias*."

"End of hallway, fire exit, up the escape, down the other side of the building?" Crow asked.

"Yeah, and quick, very quick. They coming." The clerk made no effort to say good-bye. He was there one moment and out the door, vanished, the next.

Heddy already had her clothes on. Crow was dressed and untying their hostages in the adjoining room. "Wake the hell up, get up, get your shoes on!"

Jay was wide awake, as if he had been listening the entire time. "More buddies from St. Louis?"

Crow ignored him while untying the girl. "Put your shoes on," he said. "Let's go."

In less than two or three minutes Crow had everyone out the door, the leather satchel with the money in it hanging from his shoulder like dead weight. They moved down the dimly lighted hall to the red light signaling the fire exit. Carrie took that instant to go a little crazy. She started repeating, "Let us go, let us go, let us . . ."

Heddy whacked her so hard in the back of the head with a fist that Carrie was thrown off balance and had to catch herself on the wall. "You don't move it, I'll shoot your fucking heart out."

Jay gave Heddy a hard look while he grabbed for his staggering wife and pushed her through the exit. They all stood on a dim landing, weak yellow light from a wire-caged bulb outlining stairs that went down, stairs that went up, and through the wall window, the fire escape.

"Raise that," Heddy said to Jay.

Jay pulled up the window as instructed. The sound was loud in Crow's ears.

"Now go out and climb to the top."

Jay glanced quickly at Emily as if imparting strength to her before doing as he was told. Heddy made Carrie go out next, followed by the little girl. Crow brought up the rear as Heddy moved onto the metal fire escape landing and took the rungs upward. He said, "I hate heights."

He didn't think anyone heard him and was maybe kind of glad for that.

We were in a pot of trouble that night, I told the therapist policeman as he lit another cigarette.

It was like all the other trouble rolled up into one huge cabbage head, boiling away in a big black pot, stinking like cabbage does.

The rungs were slippery with damp and there was fog crouching on top of the building like a very big, building-size gray cat. The fog scared me more than the thought of slipping off the fire escape. We couldn't see *what* might be up there on the roof. I understood there were some men looking for Heddy and Crow, and I knew they must be from the drug gangs, not the police, from the way I'd heard the clerk talking about them. My main worry was—*what if they were waiting for us to get up there on the roof?*

I felt my legs shaking as I climbed. I kept catching little looks up at the bank of fog hovering like something alive over the edge of the hotel building. In front of me was Mama, still muttering about how they needed to let us go, just let us go, *please Jesus.*

Above her was Daddy and I saw when he disappeared over the edge, swallowed into the swirl of thick fog. I paused, holding my breath, and from below me Heddy tapped at the back of one of my legs. "Get fucking moving!" she said. That scared me more than any old fog so I scrambled up another few steps until I caught up with Mama.

I didn't want Heddy mad at me, not now, not on the slippery steps.

An arm came down out of the fog, taking hold of Mama's arm, lifting her up until she too disappeared. I was about to cry. I didn't want to do that—cry. I hadn't done that hardly at all during the days we were with Heddy and Crow. I didn't cry even when I couldn't stop thinking about the young man who died in our motel room or the policeman Heddy shot, or the man down by the fishing camp, or those people in the convenience store. I thought I might never cry anymore and that meant I was grown, but now I could feel myself puddling up with tears half blinding me. That's when Daddy's strong arm reached down again and caught me, bringing me up and up onto the roof's edge and pulling me over it into the soup.

That's what it was like. Thick and wet, lukewarm soup. I could see vague outlines of Mama and Daddy, then Crow and Heddy as they piled onto the rooftop. When anyone moved, the fog parted and then swept back again, folding around him. I licked my lips and tasted salt. My tears, I guess, because I'd cried. I didn't think fog had salt in it.

Suddenly that made me mad enough I stopped crying. If anyone could have seen me clear, he'd have seen I was up on my feet standing, my hands on my hips, mad and madder yet that we had been done this way. I was angry we were still being pushed around like we were little ragdolls you put in chairs at a table for a tea party. I was no doll. I was tired of all this pushing and shoving.

"Everyone hold hands. We've got to get across this bastard to the other fire escape."

That was Crow. I almost didn't mind him, didn't do what he said, but Daddy had my hand and I couldn't pull away or I knew I'd be lost in the fog and might fall right off the edge.

It seemed forever crossing the roof, running into stacks and vents that stuck up from the floor and tripped us before we could see them. Heddy cursed beneath her breath, saying things worse than she'd ever said before. Both of them cussed all the time, but this night Heddy came up with stuff that scorched my ears.

I was about to cry again until I let the mad come back. I wouldn't cry because of her, or of being in this awful, damp, blinding fog, or of having to climb down fire escapes to keep two men from finding us. I wouldn't cry if they beat me, that's what I thought. Kid or not, I didn't have to act like one and nothing we were going through was going to make me.

One by one we found the handrails on the fire escape on the opposite side of the building, and one by one we carefully got ourselves onto it and down. Once out of the fog and back at street level where I could see again, I didn't think I'd cry, or want to cry, again.

Once on the ground, Crow said, "Do we go to the van?"

"Sometimes I think your brain's no bigger than a tadpole, honest to fucking Christ," Heddy said. "No, we don't go to the van, they could be there. We walk away from here, that's what we do, now let's go before they figure out we went over the roof."

It must have been one or one-thirty in the morning. We hadn't gotten to the hotel until a little after midnight. I was tired and sleepy, but it didn't look like we'd sleep anymore that night.

The streets were oily black with night dew, pools of light from street lamps dotting the dark. There were no cars on the streets moving and the stoplight at the corner blinked silently from red to yellow to green. I could smell the town. It was a smell like a bag of wet kittens, wet fur and burlap.

Where were we going? What would happen if I just skipped away from them? If I just took off down a side street and ducked through parking lots, losing them?

But I couldn't leave my mother. Who would she have if I left her? No one. Daddy had really deserted her now.

The clanging started up in my head that signaled someone was seeping. That's what I call it sometimes when I start picking up the thoughts from someone—their minds are seeping. I tried to block it out, but it was very loud and I guess I wasn't surprised to find out it was Crow; the thoughts belonged to him. They were strong and noisy, a herd of wild horses stomping down through canyons like in old cowboy movies.

Most of it was too mixed up crazy to understand, but one thought of his stood out. *He had the money, all the money, and he'd kill anyone who tried to take it away.*

Especially if that someone was Daddy.

★ ★ ★ ★ ★

It was the first time Heddy had found herself unable to cope. As the five of them trooped along the dark sidewalk away from the area of the hotel, she slipped her hand into her bag and brought out a bottle. Needed just a sip, that's all, something to steady her.

A sip didn't do it. She drank deeper, longer, fire burning the back of her throat and it seemed even her gums tingled and her tongue caught flame. She paused to catch her breath, stopping on the sidewalk to blink and to collect herself. Crow turned around, scowling.

"What are you doing?" he asked. Then he saw the bottle in her hand. "This is no time for that!"

"Don't tell me what time it is or what I can do," she snapped, putting the Jim Beam to her mouth and swallowing a third time. She could feel it working already. A new sun sank into her belly and lit her from inside out. It was like swallowing a nuclear reactor. She even stood straighter and everything took on a supernatural sheen, coming into sharp relief. She could get on with the world now. She could handle whatever it sent her, C.O.D. or Federal Express; she was ready for it.

Crow grabbed her elbow and pulled her along the sidewalk. "Get moving," he told the Anderson family who had stopped, impeding his path.

"Let me go." Heddy said it so softly she wasn't sure he had heard her.

He did let go of her arm, however. He said, "Don't get yourself drunk, Heddy, we have to get out of here."

Heddy looked behind them. They had turned a few times since leaving the back of the hotel building, but she could still see the three-story structure against the night sky. No one was on the street. It was as eerie as being lost in a Twilight Zone episode.

"This place is so empty, it spooks me," she said. "Where are all the people? Are they all sleeping?"

"Just hold it together. We'll find somewhere else to hole up till morning."

"Which the hell way is Mexico?" she asked.

"I have no idea. We can't do anything until daylight."

They wove through the small town streets like children on an illicit lark, taking corners without knowing where they led, moving away from the heart of the business district to the dry edge of the city, always alert to passing vehicles and shadows that followed behind them. Most of Brownsville was spread out from the center and littered with franchises—fast foods, sports wear, shoe stores, massive warehouses. The city had grown over the years, leaching out toward the desert north and west. To the east, however, the lights ended much sooner, the businesses petered out, the warehouses disappeared.

They were nearly to the dark and empty city limits when Heddy felt the repercussions of her drinking. The alcohol made her head swim so that she staggered, missing a step and nearly falling headlong onto her face. Crow caught and righted her, hissing through his teeth.

Hell, she *was* drunk! What a grand thing to be. She usually could drink much more than the few ounces she'd swallowed minutes before and not be affected in the least. But this time the street and the parked cars and the lights kept wavering to remind her she was not altogether sober.

It must have been the adrenaline, she decided, the flight from the hotel, the fear of a showdown with two more toughs dogging them all the way across the south from Missouri. That combined with the alcohol sent her reeling. She had to hold onto Crow for support, which raised her ire. "You got us into this," she accused. "It's all your fault."

"I fucking did not," he said.

"Yes, you did. Don't think I don't know you had something waiting at that hotel. I know. And those assholes from the lab house knew too. You're about as dumb as a wrecking yard." She giggled at that, though it wasn't very funny. Crow being stupid was not funny.

"Whatta you mean I had something waiting?" He sounded all wounded and peeved. It made her want to sock him.

"The money," she said and noticed the words slurred together despite her best efforts. It came out sounding like "Uhmoney."

"You're drunk."

"I'm not stupid though."

"You're stupid drunk."

She pulled away from his hand and hauled back on her heels. She was nearly shouting. "You weren't going to tell me you sent the rest of the money here! You lying, cheating-ass bucket of piss."

"Hold on, Heddy . . ."

They were all standing in the middle of an empty street crossing, watching The Heddy Show. She knew it, could see it as if she were standing back and watching too. She knew she was being bad, she was going straight to hell this way, but Crow made her so mad she could reach down and yank off his dick. He was trying to skim her. After what she'd done for him.

"After what I did for you!" she screamed.

"Now, stop it, take it easy, hush now . . ."

He approached her, trying to take her arms, but she pushed him away and fell back, catching herself just before she fell. "You don't lay your maggot hands on me, buster."

Crow laughed. That made her so furious she wanted to roar and fall rolling to the street. "There was six hundred thousand in that kitchen," she said in a controlled voice so that she would not stutter, intent on getting it out in the open. "Six hundred thousand! And you ship it down here for safe-keeping to that rat-hole hotel and you weren't gonna tell me."

"If you keep this up, someone's going to hear you." Crow glanced around at the middle-of-the-night emptiness and shivered. "What if those guys come cruising through here and see us in the middle of the goddamn street? What if someone calls the cops?"

The mention of the law made her eyes squint. She knew he was right, something in the back of her head said listen to him, he's right, get your ass out of here, but his betrayal was so large, so fresh, so . . . so . . . unfair. . . .

Tears broke and rushed down her face. She swatted at her cheeks to keep the tears at bay. "I wouldn't have stolen from you," she said in a small, sad voice. "I was the one worked out how to get you out of prison. I've done everything for you. . . ."

Crow came closer and took her arm again. "C'mon, let's find somewhere to get off the street, we'll talk then."

"I want to go home," Carrie said. The Andersons had been quiet all this time, watching the spectacle of Heddy losing her famous cool.

Heddy looked at her and said, "Is she who you want to run off with to spend that money?"

Crow denied it and told her to keep moving, don't talk about it, this was nuts.

She sneaked her hand into her bag again and, turning her head to the left so Crow couldn't see, she took another slug of the whiskey. If she was going to be drunk, by God, she was going to be freaking out-of-this-world drunk, she was going to be walking-in-a-dream drunk, she was going to be *so drunk* she wouldn't even remember herself.

It might have taken them an hour of steady walking, but they found themselves outside of Brownsville on the outskirts where Mexican families lived in small tract houses on tiny plots of desert land. An occasional flower box full of geraniums lightened up an otherwise drab home here and there, but most of the houses were run down and sad as wilted daisies. There were rusted cars up on concrete blocks, broken toys hiding like soldiers in tall weeds, and dog-chewed scatters of garbage in the tablet-size front yards.

Crow hustled them all past this and through it to the edge of the development, Heddy complaining all the way. He had to get them away from town, away from habitation, though he didn't quite know where he was headed. Now and again he made them stop while he checked parked cars at the curbside for one with a key left in it, but no luck. Even owners of broken-down ten-year-old cars weren't cavalier enough to leave their keys in the ignition. This was a changed world. There just wasn't any faith anymore, unluckily. He could try to hotwire a car, but that was a really chancy prospect, what with all the new ignition systems and the alarms and such.

When the little girl, Emily, started lagging back, he knew he wouldn't be holding his little group together much longer. They must have walked for miles and hadn't seen but two other living beings in passing cars gliding ghost-like down the streets.

He must find them somewhere to rest. If he didn't find someplace safe soon, he thought there would be a revolt. Either Heddy would drop over drunk in the gutter, Jay would make a break for it, or the little girl might sit down and refuse to move again. And he sure as hell wasn't going to carry her.

It was that kind of night, after all. Things going all wrong, going all to hell. All he could think about was the guys back in St. Louis had tracked his movements to the motel he and Heddy stayed in the night after the murders and the robbery of the loot. Could they have then had a tail on him when he dropped the manila package in the mailbox? If they could have fished it out, they wouldn't have had to track them down here, having recovered the main amount of what had been stolen from them.

Unless they'd watched him closely, how could they have known what hotel . . . ? He remembered then the van and how they'd let the one guy live at the abandoned fishing camp up in the middle of Texas. That man knew the van. They simply tracked it down, the goddamn van. It made him want to slap his head in wonder at how stupid they'd been.

Shit. It was like he and Heddy had been dropping a trail

of crumbs all the way. If they'd only tried harder to find another car to take. They had *known* the assholes wouldn't give up trying to recover the money.

Hell. If only they hadn't picked up this fucking family who were a noose around their necks. If only he'd been straight with Heddy.

If only he had Evel Knieval's son's motorcycle and about one tenth his courage, he'd jump the fountain in Vegas.

That made him smile. It was not all lost, that was the point he needed to keep in mind. They'd gotten out of the hotel and evaded what surely would have been their deaths. He had a lot to smile about.

If only he could find a place to lie down until dawn. The muscles in the back of his neck were so tense and bunched, when he turned his head he felt like a mannequin just coming to life.

The housing development ended abruptly on the edge of a flat field hemmed by barbed wire. Ahead Crow could see one more house sitting by itself, a silhouette in the distance. It was an old white frame farmhouse set apart from the field by a ring of tall leafy trees. No lights. No cars, either, as far as he could tell.

"We head over there," he said, pushing Jay in the small of his back and hauling Heddy along by one of her arms. He had never seen her so ditzed. He thought if he let go of her, she'd fall flat on her ass in the road.

No dog barked as they moved up the rutted dirt road toward the house hidden in the trees. Thank goodness for that, Crow thought. He didn't trust or like dogs, would have shot every damn mongrel he met if left up to him.

One time when he was sixteen he'd been robbing what he took to be an empty house. A big black mongrel with a face like a Mack truck came out of nowhere and bit him in

198

the thigh, hanging on for dear life. It hurt like a motherfucker. He'd had to slam the dog in the forehead with his flashlight over and over again to get him to loosen his hold. He had the scars to prove it. Since then he had no more use for dogs than he had for a hole in his head.

There were no lights on in the house and still no evidence of a vehicle. The closer they came, the more it seemed to Crow that the house was deserted. He was sure of it when they entered the circle of trees and could see the tall rectangular windows that blinked wide curtainless eyes at the stragglers in the front yard. The door stood open to the night and any stray creatures that wished to make it home.

He breathed a sigh of relief. He thought if he had to get involved with any more hostages at this point, he'd go berserk and kill the whole goddamn bunch. He was so tired of everyone, including Heddy, that if a magic carpet had shown up at that moment, he would have climbed on it and flown off into the desert night sky.

"No one lives here," Jay said, hesitating at the edge of the weedy yard.

"Aren't we lucky sons of bitches?" Crow said, prodding the man forward. "Get your ass in there."

"This doesn't look like Mexico," Heddy complained bitterly, looking around the weed patch and swaying at the end of where he held her arm. "This *does not* look like fucking Mexico. They have *palm trees* in Mexico."

Crow let out an exasperated sound, a cross between a raspberry and a sigh. "It's just a place to stay until there's light," he said. "C'mon, Heddy, let's go inside, you can get some sleep."

"I don't woan sleep."

"Yes, you do, trust me."

199

"I wouldn't trust you to wipe mud off my shiny white ass, Crow."

He ignored her bad temper and hustled the Andersons ahead of him up the worn steps to a small porch, and in through the sagging door.

It was just awful. That was his first thought and it was born out on closer inspection. Mexicans must have used it for a layover from the illegal trek over the Rio Grande. There were bottles and cans, used baby diapers, even piles of human excrement dotted with toilet paper in the corners.

"God," he muttered, his eyes adjusting to the gloom. It reminded him too much of some of the places he had to call home when he was a kid on the run. He'd stayed in warehouses, condemned buildings, rat- and roach-infested apartments where the ceilings had holes large enough that you could see the stars and make out the Milky Way.

"Looks like your kind of place," Jay said.

"Looks like your graveyard, man." Crow pushed him once more to make his point before guiding Heddy over to a wall where he lowered her to the floor.

"Pick a spot and go to sleep or just keep quiet," he told the family. "I'll have good news for you in the morning."

"Such as?" Jay wanted to know.

"Will you let us go then?" Carrie asked.

It was Emily that Crow looked at when he let the news out. She had been staring at him the whole time, all the way down the driveway and into the house, just as if she was puzzled by what he was going to do with them. Now was the time to let her know. She was just a kid, after all, none of this was her fault.

"Yes," he stated simply, still speaking to the girl. "Tomorrow me and Heddy light out for the border and you're free to go."

"Why not tonight?" Carrie asked.

He turned from Emily to her mother. "If you have to ask that, you're not as smart as I thought you were. Now sit down and alla you shut up."

He heard the swish of liquid from behind him and knew Heddy was at the bottle again.

Goddamn her.

* * * * *

Wound up, unable to stop, like someone popped new batteries into her. The Energizer Bunny. That's what I thought about how Heddy got going that night in the farmhouse. It wasn't long till dawn. My eyes were tired and felt scratchy, and I was thirsty. I thought I could put my head in Daddy's lap and go to sleep, but Heddy had been drinking like crazy. Once she started talking, it was like a river washing over us. Even Crow couldn't get her to stop.

"You think this house is bad? Hell." She slurped from the bottle, emptied it, and threw it across the room where it slid and hit the wall. She rummaged in her purse and brought out another bottle, a full, unopened one. When Crow tried to take it from her, she took a swing at him. He put up his hands in surrender and said, "Okay, fine, drink that shit till your eyes fall out for all I care."

"I guess you think I'm gonna tell you about all the dumps I've had to live in. Well, I'm not!" Heddy said. "You think I'm pissed off my mother's husband hit me so hard in the face I can't even move half my mouth. Well, I am! I've been pissed off ever since. That's how I live—pissed off and pissed on. He got a dull knife through his ribs for it, though, so I figured it evens out. People like you . . ." She waved her hands at us and made a face before taking another swig from the new bottle. ". . . People like you feel sorry for people like me, but I'm here to tell you you're dead, you're walking-around dead people. At least I've lived a little."

"Take it easy, Heddy," Crow whined. He had moved closer to her and now sat cross-legged not far away. His gaze kept shifting between Heddy and us where we were huddled together near the center of the open room—the only area not littered with trash.

Moonlight spilled across the floor like a silver river coming through the door. I couldn't see it, the moon, but it had to be out there just above the edge of the trees. I wondered if it was a full moon, a bad loony moon. It had to be.

I shivered from the damp air and scooted over closer to my father. He hadn't been saying much at all and neither had Mama. Now that Crow had promised to set us free once it was morning, we could all stop worrying about it. There was no reason for them to hurt us. Even when we told they'd gone into Mexico, no one would ever find them, and I'd heard Heddy say there was no extradition treaty for capital crimes in Mexico. No one could touch them.

But was my Daddy still going too? He'd said he was.

While Heddy ranted on about her sorry life, I looked at Daddy from the sides of my eyes. Would he really leave us? For Heddy? For drunken and full-of-hate, messed up, murderous Heddy?

I closed my eyes to shut out Heddy's voice. I felt a purple wave of sadness coming off her. Once it touched me, I'd be swamped under all those feelings like under a big wave coming into shore from an ocean. What did Daddy think of her now that he could see her drunk and disorderly just like the people he put in jail?

My eyes flew open and I turned my head to stare straight at my father. He was crazy about her! I had picked that up like a radio picking up a strong station for just a second or two before it fades out again. He wasn't disgusted by her drinking like the rest of us were. He thought she was exciting, she was unpredictable, he thought. She was very dark and scary, like a storm cloud filled with streaks of lightning. He was . . . he was . . . I don't know how to say this except to just say it. She turned him on.

My father wanted her for his lover, drinking or not, deformed mouth or not, criminal or not.

Then information came to me that made my head reel. Heddy wasn't the first woman he'd liked this way. There had been others, women from the street in our town, even women on the police force, women Mama never knew about. A lot of women, some of them almost as dangerous as Heddy.

I wished I'd never found that out. It made me so unhappy that I wanted to cry again.

I moved away from Daddy. I didn't want to be near my father anymore. I made up my mind never to meddle in his thoughts again. If he wanted Heddy that much, he was lost to us anyway. Mama sure didn't need him.

He had been cruel to her; I understood that really for the first time that night. How cruel he'd been. He might have been my father, but I stopped loving him like one that night once I knew he was no better than the two people who had kept us prisoner so many days. He was just a criminal of another sort. All his crimes were hidden away under cover. He beat his wife, he went to bed with strange women, and he would break the law and give up his family for the love of money and the promise of wild sex with Heddy.

". . . Even Crow doesn't know about my life, not really," Heddy was saying. When he tried to protest, she shushed him real loud with a finger to her lips.

"And Crow don't know me too damn much because if he did, he wouldn't have tried hiding most of the money from me."

Before Crow could say anything else, Heddy felt around in her big purse again and produced her gun. She didn't wait to aim it, but waved it high. She pulled the trigger, shooting above Crow's head. The shot filled the house, the burst of fire from the cylinder and the noise made us all jump and let out scared noises. The smell from the gunfire caused my nose to wrinkle up and I put my hand over it.

Mama grabbed my hand and pulled me under her arms. "Please don't," she said. She was crying and her voice was all wavy and trembly.

"Hell, what're you doing, Heddy?" Crow got to his feet and moved halfway across the room from her. "Someone will hear that."

"Someone will hear that," she mimicked and fired again, this time to her right, at the wall. Plaster splattered onto the floor.

My ears were ringing. I wished we could get out of the house, run for the door, and disappear across the field toward the other houses where we could find some help. Crow promised us we could go free in the morning, but here we were in terrible danger just before we could get away from them. Heddy had gone crazy, that's what had happened. The whiskey made her careless and mean.

"Heddy, put down the gun." Daddy also came to his feet and took a step toward her.

"This motherfucker tried to screw me out of the money," she said, waving the gun at Crow.

"I know, I know, but shooting him now won't solve the problem. You keep shooting and someone might call the authorities."

"I swear to God, Heddy, I was gonna tell you." Crow looked ready to bolt for the door.

She shot in his direction, and he danced around the floor like he would be able to dodge the bullet. Heddy laughed and lowered the gun to the floor, her head hanging. "I ought to shoot his guts out."

"You can have the money!" Crow hurried to his leather bag and pulled out a thick manila envelope that he threw over to Heddy. "Goddamnit, I was just keeping it safe for us."

Heddy started to laugh louder. "You don't think I'd get it? You think giving it to me now makes it all right again?" She raised the gun. "I'm going to kill you, Crow. You deserve it, don't you, you little creep?"

"Shit, Heddy, stop messing around. . . ."

She squeezed off another shot and Crow fell down on the floor. I screamed. I thought he was dead and I was afraid to look, but I couldn't help myself. He had fallen on his butt and then over to one side. He sat up slowly. He said, "Don't kill me, Heddy. Please don't. I'm sorry. I'm sorry I took the money without telling you."

The gun in Heddy's hand wavered. I heard her crying and looked at her. I didn't think she ever cried. All this time with them and I could never imagine her crying like other people.

She dropped the gun with a clatter on the wood boards of the floor. She brought both hands to her face and wept into them. It was so pitiful. I didn't want to feel sorry for her, but I couldn't help it. She was scary, she was crazy, she was drunk, and she was a killer. But now she was crying like a little kid, her shoulders all hunched over and shaking. Pity came into my heart and swelled it until tears came into my own eyes.

At that moment it could have all been over. Daddy was closer to Heddy than Crow and if he'd wanted, he could have stepped closer and taken the gun from the floor. Crow didn't have a gun out. Daddy could have ended it all right there, by taking control. He could have held them prisoner, turned the tables on them, and turned them into the law.

But he didn't.

I looked up at him, waiting, mentally urging him to do it, to do the right thing, to end all this. At the same time I understood what opportunity he had let go by, Crow finally realized it too. He scrambled forward on hands and knees and snatched the gun lying in front of Heddy. He rolled onto his back and pointed it at Daddy. "You get back," he said. "Sit down over there."

I'll never know what was going through Daddy's head right then. It was like he didn't want to be the boss. He didn't want to straighten it all out and take Crow and Heddy into custody.

Of course he didn't. He wanted to go to Mexico with them. Mexico, land of palm trees and freedom from the pain of his American life with his American family.

My Daddy was truly one of the bad guys. Even my mother knew it now. We all knew the whole truth now.

* * * * *

Crow cuddled Heddy in his arms and let her cry against the front of his shirt while he rocked her. He felt a bottomless well of regret brimming up from his chest into his head. In those murky waters floated all the events Heddy had survived to make it to this place along the border of Mexico. Also floating in it, rubbing against his sensitivities like spiny fish, were the things he had done and seen and overcome.

They were so much alike, the two of them. It's why they clung together, why they needed each other.

Not many times had he recalled feeling so responsible for so many wrongful deeds. In order to kill, it seemed to him, the reality of murder has to slip off and away from a person. Else he will feel answerable and too horrible to keep going without putting a bullet through his own head.

Like Heddy, he had done what he thought he had to do. When you have never been free and the possibility of freedom comes along, there is nothing to do but take it, he thought; what else could you do? Prentice told him that once while they played checkers in prison. Prentice, the jailhouse philosopher, always reading and saying stuff no one else would say. Others made fun of him for it, but Crow knew there was a kernel of truth in some of the crap Prentice said.

That's what the six hundred thousand dollars represented. Freedom for the first time in his miserable life. It was dirty money, illegal and tainted. It belonged to anybody who could keep it. Now that he had betrayed Heddy and made her cry, he could see he had done one of the worst things in all his life. He never should have mistrusted her. He shouldn't have tried to keep secrets from her. He shouldn't have been *so selfish*.

He stopped rocking and glanced over in the shadows at Jay Anderson. Heddy wanted the jerk along, but that wasn't a betrayal. To betray a person, you stole his freedom. Who you had sex with had nothing to do with it. Hadn't he done his thing in prison, hadn't he even come close to doing it with Carrie? It didn't mean he wasn't still attached like a Siamese baby to Heddy's side.

He didn't know how it was going to work out with three of them trying to keep a low profile in Mexico with that kind of money, but Heddy's wanting Jay along—and he was sure that she did—did not constitute reason to desert her.

Hell, she had every right to shoot out his guts. He didn't know what he'd been thinking, shipping off most of the money that way.

The first time he met Heddy, they'd been at a party. About twenty people were downing drugs like there was to be no tomorrow and the rest of them were getting drunk. It was loud, people spilling throughout the house into all the rooms.

He had found Heddy sitting alone in a broken wicker chair near an open back door. The sky outside was clear, sprinkled with stars. She just sat, staring up at the sky, her hands clasped together between her knees. She wore black jeans and a tight black halter-top. Pale bare skin showed between the bottom of the top and her jean waist. She was thin and ethereal, her hair hanging long around her shoulders. He remembered noticing the little black sword tattooed on her breast, the tip of it hidden by the halter. She was so cool, untouchable, a little beauty queen sitting apart, all on her own.

He had wondered, too, why she was alone, pretty girl like her. Then she raised her face to him as he came around her and to the open door and he saw something wild and unformed in her eyes. When the small smile came, it only raised half her mouth, causing her to look both grotesque and vulnerable at once. He was careful not to let his expression change. He knew instantly that any future relationship they might have hinged on his first reaction to her deformed face.

He said, "Hi there," and she told him her name. He had thought at first it was a nickname, "Heady," meaning she could make a man crazy or she gave great head, hell, what did he know, but she spelled it for him right away. "H-e-d-d-y," she said and smiled crookedly.

He had never been able to explain why this particular woman moved him. Over the next two years, before he'd been busted for nearly killing the guy in the pool hall and going to prison for it, he and Heddy lived together in a small shambles of a house in one of St. Louis' least desirable neighborhoods. They made out the best they could. When they had to steal to stay alive, Heddy never flinched; she was always right at his side, willing to take the risks.

She had brought him money to Leavenworth, saving him from having to toss the salad of every big goon in the place. She'd stuck by him. And she'd worked out the plan for his escape.

For this he had betrayed her. Hadn't trusted her. Meant to keep it all for himself.

He rocked her until she slept and then eased her down into his lap where he gently removed the curly wig from her head and brushed back the long tumbling hair from her cool temple.

God, he couldn't wait until the sun rose. They could get out of here and cross over the border, pretending they were American tourists on a little day jaunt. They'd wait until there was a crowd crossing and tag along with them as if in their party. No one ever checked the ID of a person crossing *into* Mexico. They'd hurry across the river and on the other side . . .

. . . On the other side they'd really be free forever. He and Heddy. And Jay too if that's what she wanted. He owed her the concession. He would never betray her again.

* * * * *

They had dozed, fatigue taking them one by one. They all lay curled and lying on each other—Emily with her head in her mother's lap, Carrie lying against her husband, Heddy and Crow wrapped together like snakes tangled together on the hard wood floor.

The first Crow knew there was someone else in the deserted dark house besides them was when he woke with a gun pressed hard against his skull. His eyes opened wide. He blinked and drew in a sharp breath, afraid Heddy was still furious and about to kill him.

A voice said, "You should have gone further south a lot faster. Get up."

Heddy sat up, startled, when Crow moved. She squinted at the two shadowy figures hovering over them and said, "Who the hell . . . ?"

Crow knew now that one of the cars passing them as they walked through town must have been these two men they'd fled from at the hotel. He was suddenly scared for his life. It was not the first time, but on some riotous instinctive level he knew it might really be the last.

"They just want the money, Heddy. Give it to 'em."

"What's going on?" Jay had wakened and so had his family. They all sat up in the near-dark, Emily rubbing at her eyes.

"Who are you?" The man with the gun spoke to Jay. He stood between the two groups on the floor. He flicked on a flashlight and shined it directly into Jay's face, then swept it over Carrie and Emily.

"That must be the hostages," the second man said, stepping forward. "They took them in Missouri."

"Oh yeah. You're famous," he said to Jay. "You're all over the news. They've even got the FBI out looking for you. Cop, they say. You a cop?"

"Yes."

"Not a very good one if you got stuck with these two little petty thieves without a struggle." He turned back to Crow, shining the light into his eyes.

"Hey!" Crow shielded his face with his hands.

"Where's the money? We want it and we want it now."

"Heddy's got it. In her bag."

Heddy didn't react. He was hoping she'd know what to do. The envelope he'd thrown at her earlier lay crumpled between them, covered by their legs. In that envelope Crow believed as much as four, even five, hundred thousand dollars were preserved. These guys weren't getting it unless they stepped over his dead body. He was dead anyway if they took it from him. He and Heddy could not live without it to pay off officials in Mexico. He sure as hell wasn't going down there to work in a cantina waiting tables or shining tourist shoes the rest of his freaking life.

Heddy seemed to come to life slowly, as if waking from a dream. She must have been hung over, but it didn't show except for her dreamy, slow-moving quality. She said, "I've got it. Right here."

The man with the flashlight did as Crow thought he would. He grabbed out for Heddy's bag before she could get her hand into it. While preoccupied this way, Crow carefully reached out in the darkness beside him and felt around in his own bag for the gun. He felt one, knew it was Jay's service revolver, pulled it free as quietly as possible.

Then he fell onto his back suddenly, lifted the gun, not knowing how true his aim, and he was pulling the trigger. Fire bloomed, lighting the room, once, twice, and the sound echoed off the walls like Fourth of July cherry bombs.

The man holding Heddy's purse dropped where he was standing. Heddy's bag fell with the man. The flashlight banged onto the floor, rolling wildly as the light from it skittered across the room. Crow couldn't see the man who had been behind the first he shot.

Heddy was up and moving. The whole room came alive with motion. Crow couldn't see a thing as he slid around the floor on his back, pointing the gun, afraid to shoot, afraid he'd hit Heddy or one of the Andersons. He couldn't make out who was who, didn't know where he should aim. He was breathing fast and hard; his stomach seemed so tight it would fold in on itself.

A bright burst of light blossomed from ten feet away and Crow felt something rip into his thigh. He screamed, dropping his gun. He'd been hit, goddamnit!

Someone had hands on him and he tried to lash out, but stopped in time to keep from knocking Heddy away. She felt along his body and then the floor until she found the gun.

The whole room lit up with sound and smoke. Heddy and the man with the gun spattered the darkness with rapid-fire blinks of harsh white blasts.

Crow ducked, covering his head with his arms, squirming and moaning from the scalding hot pain shooting up from his thigh. He expected to be hit again, to die here on the floor of a filthy house on the night before the door opened to real freedom. He was yelling without knowing it, "Nononononono . . . !" He was panicked to the point of insanity.

The firing ceased and the clicking of a hammer on an empty cylinder was all that remained. Crow threw off his arms from around his head and tried to see something, anything. Heddy kneeled over him, her legs against his back, and it was she who was holding out the revolver before her, clicking and clicking on dead air. She finally slumped back on her heels.

"Is he . . . ?"

Heddy said nothing. She lowered the gun and finally dropped it to the floor. Crow could now hear the little girl crying from somewhere across the room. He saw shadows entering a doorway from the back of the house. Jay said, "Is it over? Heddy? Heddy, are you all right?"

* * * * *

Daddy was the one who got the flashlight and found the dead man. The other man was hurt, but not dead. He was shot twice, once in the stomach and once in his arm. Daddy moved the flashlight beam over his body, the blood showing up like black spots against the man's clothes. He was sprawled on the floor like a baby, holding both hands over his stomach and crying now. He'd been shot in the same place as the boy at the motel days before. In his stomach.

"Help me, I'm dying," he said to Daddy.

Swinging the light away from him, Daddy rested it on Crow. Heddy was helping him to sit up. There was blood coming from his leg, staining the floor black. "You're shot," Daddy said.

"Yeah, he was hit in the leg," Heddy said. She pulled her bag over to her and drew out a tee shirt. She took it by the neck and ripped it down the center, jerking at the material and cursing when it failed to give the first couple of tries.

"I'm dying!" the man said again.

Daddy kept the light on Crow's upper leg while Heddy wrapped the shirt around it twice and tied it in a knot.

"How are you going to cross the border like that?" Daddy asked.

"Are you always so goddamn practical?" Heddy yelled.

"I'm a cop." He shrugged as if to say it was expected of cops to make practical remarks and to think ahead.

"If you're a cop, man, do something for me," the dying man said. "I'm losing too much blood."

Daddy turned back to him and stooped nearby, playing the light over his midsection. I could see how the blood had coated his hands, the slimy blood dripping off his knuckles to the floor. I cringed and turned away my face. I couldn't watch it anymore.

Daddy said, "You'd die before anyone could get you to a doctor. It's too late."

The man clenched his teeth and moaned even louder.

"Shut up!" Heddy had finished tending to Crow and now she stood up and stalked over to where the man was on the floor. "I'll put a bullet in your head if you want me to. You want me to?"

"No! Don't let her near me, don't let her do it!"

Then Heddy laughed and that was the weirdest thing to hear. There was the smell of blood everywhere and the lingering scent of the gun blasts. There was darkness except for the small pool from the flashlight that played over the man on the floor. Then Heddy's crazy laughter took hold of the room and I thought this was probably what it was like in war when people had to kill; it made everything all wrong, all crazy. People laughed when they should cry, they bled and died and there was enough hate between them to raise the devil.

I heard a gurgling sound and even though Mama held me tight, one arm around my neck, I turned my head and looked over. Daddy had the light on the man's face. He was dead. His eyes were open, but he was dead. His whole face had relaxed and gone slack. I thought dead people had closed eyes. I couldn't stop staring at the man's unblinking open eyes.

Mama hugged me to her and said softly, "Don't look, don't look, baby." She was trembling and her teeth were chattering although it was a warm night.

I heard Daddy say; "The problem remains. How are you going to get Crow across the border hurt like that?"

"You'll help him," Heddy said. "He can lean on you."

"With that bloody shirt tied around his leg? The border guards aren't blind, you know."

"You're not leaving me behind," Crow said.

"Of course not!" Heddy went to him and checked the tied shirt. She looked up at Daddy. "We'll buy some stuff at a drug store and bandage it right. I'll get him new jeans and a . . . a cane he can lean on. You'll help him cross the bridge."

I didn't hear Daddy answer, but I imagine that he nodded his head. He was part of this now. Like Crow, he did whatever Heddy said.

* * * * *

While Frank Hawkins listened to what went on in the house on the outskirts of Brownsville that night, he remembered where he had been at the time. In a private plane with two FBI agents on their way to the border city.

After picking up Craig Walker's trail south, they could see they were headed for Matamoras to cross. Early in the morning after their arrival, hysterical calls came into the city's police department. There was gunfire at an abandoned house not far from a small subdivision at the edge of town. A patrol car was sent to investigate and didn't see anything out of order. No cars, no lights, nothing. They drove on past on the road without turning in. Within two hours, more calls came in reporting a second round of gunfire coming from the same house.

This time Frank and the agents accompanied the locals in a car to check it out. They parked in the subdivision and went on foot across the pasture toward the house in the trees. Once close enough, they heard voices and knew the place needed to be staked out. They'd heard a child's voice. They weren't going to rush in during the middle of night, in the dark, and put her in harm's way.

This called for careful work. It meant they needed to regroup and think it over. Leaving a patrolman at the subdivision's edge with a radio, they returned downtown and made plans. They needed men, a swat crew. They needed a negotiator. They'd have to call in some help.

Before daybreak, they had it.

* * * * *

With dawn came the sound of a bullhorn commanding they come out with their hands raised.

Crow must have slept a bit because at the noise he fairly leaped out of his skin as if roused by shouts from a monstrous dream. "What?"

The others moved and came fully awake, everyone speaking at once.

Jay didn't even look as if he had slept. He hurried to one of the windows. "It's the police."

"What the fuck . . . ?" Heddy struggled up, licking her bottom lip and looking pale and hung over.

The little girl said, "Daddy, will they shoot us?"

"Oh God, they've surrounded the house," Carrie said.

"Take it easy, hold on," Crow said. "Heddy, help me onto my feet. The rest of you move away from the door."

Outside the sun poured brilliant splashes of light through the trees. Beyond the overgrown, weedy yard stood a line of patrol cars, lights blinking obscenely in the new sunshine. Crow leaned on Heddy's shoulder. They could see some kind of tactical team dressed in riot gear—helmets, jackets, and high-powered rifles—a whole force of men peeking from behind fenders and hoods and tree trunks.

Crow moved back and through the house, finding his way to the rear with Heddy's help. The kitchen was in back and a bolted door to the outside. He peered through the dusty windows and didn't see anything, but that didn't mean they weren't out there somewhere.

"See anyone?" Heddy asked, a tremor in her voice.

"Nah. Nobody. Stay cool now."

His mouth was dry and his stomach clenched into a knot. His leg burned like it was on fire. Every time he took a step, pain shot up into his groin. He didn't even know if the bullet was still in his thigh or if it had passed through the flesh.

He finally realized someone had heard the shooting and called in the cops. Maybe their friends from St. Louis, the two men lying dead on the floor in the front room, had won after all. It wouldn't, by God, surprise him to learn that's how they were trapped—trying to save their lives, they had forfeited them.

He hurried to the front room again. Heddy let him lean against the wall near the window. She began nervously re-filling her gun's cartridge clip. She kept dropping shells and saying, "Oh shit, oh shit."

"What are we gonna do, Heddy?" It was as if his brain had skipped. There seemed to be two alternatives, give it up and walk out or take a stand, neither of which appeared to be actions he could indulge. Surrender his life into the state's hands again? Or shoot it out with a squad that out-numbered them five to one? It was a fucking western, is what it was. It was high noon in Brownsville, Texas, the problem being he was no Gary Cooper.

"I didn't see anyone in the back," she said.

"No, but they might be hiding in the weeds or behind the trees out there."

"Okay, we tell them we have hostages. We have a kid in here." She scowled at the girl. "We get them busy in the front and then we break for it out the back."

He hadn't wanted her to say that. "Hell, Heddy . . ."

"WHAT DO YOU WANT TO DO?"

Her shout shocked him enough to make him flinch and hunker his shoulders. "I don't know."

"You don't ever fucking know. That's why you need me. Now take this gun and watch that window." She pointed to the one right of the door. She moved quickly to the opposite window on the left.

"Craig Walker! Harriet Arnold! You have five minutes to come out with your hands behind your head!" shouted the voice over the bullhorn.

"Listen to them," Jay said quietly. "I don't see a way out of this."

Heddy whirled around. "You better find a way out of it or you're going to be just as dead as we are."

"If you'll let Carrie and Emily go out, I'll help you," he said.

"No fucking way." She turned back to the window and suddenly smashed out a lower pane of glass with the gun. To Crow she looked like someone gone mad. There was a darkness in her eyes that meant real business this time. He'd seen her this way just before they took the lab house and if she'd not been on his team, it would have scared him to death.

"We've got three hostages in here!" she shouted. "There's a family. The kid's ten years old. You want to talk to me about that, you want to negotiate this thing?"

Heddy waited, glancing over at Crow, and once back to Jay. Crow hugged the wall near the window, gun in hand, afraid to look out there, afraid a marksman would have him in his scope dead on.

"Send out the woman and child, then we'll negotiate,"

the man with the bullhorn yelled.

"You must think we're idiots!" Heddy pointed the gun out the broken pane and pulled the trigger carefully.

That's when all hell broke loose.

★ ★ ★ ★ ★

Crow never would have believed a tactical team would open fire on a house filled with hostages. As the gunfire was returned when Heddy pulled the trigger, all he could think was that some hothead on the team got out of control and started off the shooting, the rest just followed.

Bullets riddled the walls so that they all had to hit the floor on their faces. Windows burst, shattering glass over them. Everyone was screaming, Heddy, Carrie, Emily. Even Jay was shouting furiously how they couldn't do this, *they weren't supposed to do this!*

Crow saw Jay crawl over to the window where Heddy lay. "Give me a gun," he yelled. She brought out a gun one of the two men had been packing who caught them sleeping earlier.

Jay got to his knees to peek out the window. He said, "Carrie, Em, stay down."

He said to Heddy, "C'mon, you wanted a fight, you've got one."

She looked up at him as she might look at a hero and got to her knees, then to her feet. "Let's do it," she said. "Fuck it."

Crow moved back to his own window and, trembling like a man with palsy, raised his gun to the frame.

* * * * *

In the first barrage of gunfire, I think I realized if I stayed in the house, I'd die. Oh, well, don't apologize for those men, it wouldn't have mattered what they did at that house, it was all going sour the minute they showed up. I guess I should say it all went bad when we stopped in at the Long Horn Caverns and got hooked up with Heddy and Crow.

"It got out of hand," Mr. Hawkins said sadly. "The hostage negotiator was on his way from Houston. Orders were not to fire because they knew you were in there, they knew there were hostages. But once Heddy starting firing, it was all over. A hothead riot cop who hadn't been in the unit but two weeks lost it and started the whole thing."

Well, I said, it was a terrible thing, but Heddy wouldn't have let us come out without a fight. During the next session of gunfire, Mama was hit. We were holding one another, trying to stay down. I don't know where the bullet came from or how it found her, but it did. I had my arms around her waist, my head buried in her lap when she was struck. She fell back, letting me go, trying to catch herself. She must have cried out, but with all the noise I didn't hear her.

I felt her arms come away from me and I started to sit up to see what was wrong. There was a blank look on her face. I screamed, "Mama!" as she toppled onto the floor on her side. I tried to turn her over to see where she'd been hit. No one even knew about it except me. Daddy was busy at the window being an outlaw, helping his new partners.

221

There was blood on Mama's chest and although her eyes were still open and blinking, I knew she was probably going to die. I leaped up and ran for the door. I didn't know what I was doing anymore. I pulled the door back and I heard Daddy yell at me to *stop, wait,* but I was already outside on the little porch and flying down the steps, and then I was crossing the yard while all around me everyone was shooting at everyone else. I had my arms up in the sky and I was crying, "My Mama, my Mama's hurt!"

I know now it was a really dumb thing I did. I could have been killed easy. I wasn't thinking, I wasn't even afraid. I had to get help for her, that's all I could think about, I had to get out of the house and get help or she'd die.

Mr. Hawkins lit up a new cigarette. He inhaled before saying, "You're a brave little girl, Emily. A remarkable girl."

I wanted to tell him bravery had nothing to do with it. He didn't understand. My mother was all I had left. If I lost her, I'd have nobody.

Jay stopped firing when he saw his daughter racing across the ground between the house and the police cars. He felt his heart surge up to the roof of his mouth as he raised the barrel of the gun to the ceiling and watched, horrified and breathless, as Emily shot across the firing range. When she made it without being killed, when she was grabbed by one of the officers in charge who had been taking cover behind the back fender of one of the cars, and when she was dragged behind the car to cover and safety, he let out his breath. It had happened so fast that he still couldn't believe he'd seen it.

"That little bitch!" Heddy screamed. "Goddamn it!"

Jay turned from the window to find out where his wife was. Was she too going to follow Em out the door into the hail of bullets? A second shock traveled through his system as he took in her prone position on the floor and the blood that covered the front of her blouse. "Shit," he mumbled, going down to his hands and knees to crawl over to her.

"Jay? Jay, get back over here!"

He ignored Heddy's command. Carrie had been hit. Maybe she was dead.

"Jay!"

Heddy's scream finally got through to him and he halted halfway across the floor and turned back. He had made his pact with the woman. With the devil. He had made his pact with the devil and there was no going back now.

He reclaimed his spot at the window in time to see Crow crawl across the floor toward Carrie. He looked away. Let Heddy handle him, the betraying son of a bitch.

Crow reached her body and grabbed hold of the front of her bloody shirt, ripping it open. The wound pumped blood from just below the bra line under her left breast. *Lung*, he thought. He saw her chest heaving and saw that her mouth was wide open. She was trying to suck in enough air to stay alive.

He twisted and shouted, "Carrie's hit! She's going to die

if we don't get her out of here."

"Fuck her," Heddy said. She jerked around the window frame and fired off two shots before hiding again.

"Let's try going out the back while they have the kid," Crow said. "We gotta get outta here, Heddy. Now!"

Heddy looked at him and the oddest look came over her face. It was as if she only now really saw him near Carrie's body and the sight sickened her. She ducked and crab-walked to where he knelt. "C'mon, we're going."

Crow glanced down at Carrie; his gaze riveted on her struggling face.

"Okay," he said finally, moving away from the bleeding woman.

"I'm telling you one last time, Jay," Heddy called to Jay where he crouched at the window. "We're leaving. It's our only chance. You coming?"

Jay dropped suddenly to the floor and crawled over to join them. "Yeah, I'm coming," he said, avoiding looking at his wounded wife.

Heddy gestured to Crow and they made for the kitchen and the back door there.

The gunfire still came from the front of the house, no one there realizing the people trapped in the house were on their way out.

Crow thought he knew the future when he saw the kid run out the door into the gunfire. They'd all be dead before the sun ever got up to the middle of the sky that day. A premonition? No, it was simple enough to realize what was coming for him.

When Carrie went down, Crow knew then that the whole thing was falling apart. His suggestion that he and Heddy go out the back was a last desperate attempt to sidestep what he knew was going to happen. They were not going to be able to hold off a whole squad of cops in riot gear. They'd already emptied three of the guns. He didn't tell Heddy, but his own gun was hitting on an empty clip.

And what good was Jay? He was like some stoned motherfucking chimpanzee walking around dazed or something. He did what Heddy said, but he didn't seem to have anything left behind his eyes, like he was dead already and he knew it.

Crow also didn't really believe the cops didn't have the back covered. They had to be out there, waiting, biding their time. Sharpshooters, no doubt, stationed behind the trees or lying in cover in the swaying tall, dead grass of the field.

When up against the wall all he knew to do was what he had to do. His whole damn life it was like that, doing what he had to do, going where he had to go, taking down who he had to take down. And now he would die, he was sure of it, the way he had to die. No return to Leavenworth for him. No more cells, guards, and self-serving bastard cons. It was no kind of life, prison, death being preferable. Besides, this time they'd ask for the death sentence and they'd get it. He was in by-God Texas where they whacked a dozen death row inmates a month with lethal injections. By-God Texas loved death row. They loved whacking out the killers littering their state. What was the goddamn difference if he died today or a year from today? He'd hate to see by-God Texas have the privilege when he could handle it himself, today, right now.

At the back door, just before Heddy went ahead of him through it, he drew her back and into the circle of his arms. She smelled of fear-sweat. He buried his face in the crook of her neck, rubbing his face against her skin, taking her sweat onto him. He remembered briefly that it was at the back door of another house a lifetime in the past and a world away when he met her and they'd joined their fates. If he'd known it would have led him here, would he have taken her home that night?

Yeah, he expected he would have. What could have been better or led to any happier a place than by her side?

"We have to go," she said, pushing him away.

The gunfire had stopped and a solemn waiting silence had settled over the house. Suddenly they both flinched as they heard the voice on the bullhorn say, "Come out. No one will shoot. Surrender now and send out the hostages first."

Crow rummaged in his leather bag, digging deep beneath the manila envelope of money. He brought out the last of his crystal meth, ripped open the foil, and stuffed the crystals in his mouth. He tongued it from behind his molars, pushing all of it underneath his tongue where it bulged out his lower lip. It was the only time in his life he wished he had a way to shoot it straight into his veins.

"You ready?" Heddy asked.

The sunlight glittered off her sandy hair and from the surface of her mad eyes. God, Crow thought, she's the toughest woman on earth. She's a goddamn goddess.

"Yeah," he said. "Let's get out of here."

He pushed her behind him and went out the door first, leaping over the steps to the hard dry ground. He let out a grunt from the pain that ran up his leg from the gunshot wound there. He turned to put out his hand and just had the tips of Heddy's fingers in his palm when he realized she was pointing her gun at his heart. "Aw, Heddy . . ." he said. "Aw, hell, Heddy. . . ."

"You never should have gone to see about that woman in there, Crow. You never should have kept the money secret from me."

She pulled the trigger and the blast hit him in the center of his chest, knocking him back onto his heels where he staggered to remain upright. He thought the sky had opened because now lightning crackled and thunder filled his body from all sides. They were shooting at him from the trees, dancing him against his will away from Heddy. He twitched and jerked with each shot that entered his body, turning round and round like a wind-up toy. He screamed in agony and called out over and over, "HeddyHeddyHeddyHEDDY . . . !"

But she was gone, already out of his field of vision, suffering the same pain as he somewhere on her own away from him.

Dying hurt worse than he could have imagined. It was a shitty thing to happen to a guy.

* * * * *

The gunshots peppered Heddy's entire front from neck to groin, sending her sprawling back onto the steps, her head lying in the open doorway.

227

Jay had frozen where he'd landed on the ground, shocked at Heddy's shooting of Crow, and then mesmerized further when the shots opened from the trees that sent Crow flopping around like a downed bird. He turned back just in time to see Heddy take her first shots to the chest and then he was all motion, moving up the steps again, trying to stop what was happening by shielding her, but by the time he reached the top step she had fallen back and he was the one taking the gunfire now, stray shots meant for Heddy that bore into his back like hot drills, knocking his breath from him, knocking his life from him, knocking the world off its axis. He stumbled. He noticed the gunfire had halted again and an eerie silence filled his ears with white noise. He stared down at Heddy's dead face before he dropped to his knees, understanding pain, understanding death, wishing he was back home again, driving his patrol car, wishing for a better life. He thought of his family, lost a long time ago, lost for good now. And Heddy, gone, gone before he ever really got to be with her. He squeezed shut his eyes on the pain and rolled off the wooden steps to the ground, all the world turning to black.

Frank stood from behind his desk and put out his cigarette butt in the overflowing ashtray. Ashes were knocked onto the desktop. He pushed aside the ashtray and raked the ashes into his hand. He said to Emily as he dropped the ashes into the trash can at the side of the desk, "I'm sorry about your father."

Emily glanced down at her hands. She still had the rock she'd taken from the ground behind the police car. It was this nice man who had stepped into the open and, grabbing her, took her to the ground and safety. She rolled the stone over and rubbed it carefully as if it might eventually glow with magic. There was a ruby vein in the stone running through the brown that reminded her of blood.

"I'm sorry too," she said. "He was only bad for a little while. He wasn't always bad."

The psychologist cleared his throat and moved to her chair. He held out his hand to help her rise. "I'll have someone take you back to the hospital to see about your mother."

"Thank you."

"Emily?"

"Uh huh?" She slipped the rock into the pocket of her shorts.

"I think you saved your mother's life."

Emily started to shake her head, but she stopped. She didn't know if it was true but it was okay that he said it. None of it mattered now. "She's going to be all right."

"And so are you."

She looked up into the kindly Captain Kangaroo face and smiled a little sad smile. "Yes, I will. I'll be fine now."

"And Emily?"

"Yessir?"

"Thanks for staying so long to tell me how it happened. We couldn't make it out, a cop's family held hostage that long. It would have remained a mystery without your help to get at the truth of it."

"You don't have to tell the newspapers, do you? About Daddy and all?"

"No, I won't tell them. It's for my files and no one gets to see those."

"Good." She walked to the door and opened it, looking back over her shoulder, pausing.

"What is it?" he asked. "Have you forgotten something?"

"No, I was just checking." She smiled and pointed to her head. "Just checking."

Frank smiled back, thinking, *That's some kid, what a great kid that is, and she really reads minds too. I think she really does. Christ.*

Emily listened to those last thoughts, committed them to memory, then shut the door behind her and went with the police lady who was to drive her to the hospital.

She never looked back. She never had to. Mr. Hawkins knew everything finally, so she didn't have to live with it anymore. He knew the whole story, the terrible secrets, and all the sad deaths. She had given it away, the way you do when you have a best friend you can tell everything to. Those days on their bad trip south were all his now and she was free at last to start life new again. Her mother would take her back home to North Carolina. They'd return home safely in an airplane. Maybe at home, where accidental chaos hardly ever reared its head and life was very seldom a thing to fear, they'd be safe again.

Safe, she thought happily. Just like they said in baseball—home safe.

Author Bio

Billie Sue Mosiman is an Edgar and Stoker nominated author of a dozen novels, numerous short stories, and the co-editor of several anthologies. A native of Alabama, Mosiman has lived in Texas for many years. Most of her fiction is set in the South that she loves and understands so well. Her work reflects the dark side of the criminal mind and the psychological interactions between people in crisis. Mosiman lives on a small East Texas ranch with her husband and a little dog named Gidget.